# The Virtue of Vices

By

Jeremy McShurley

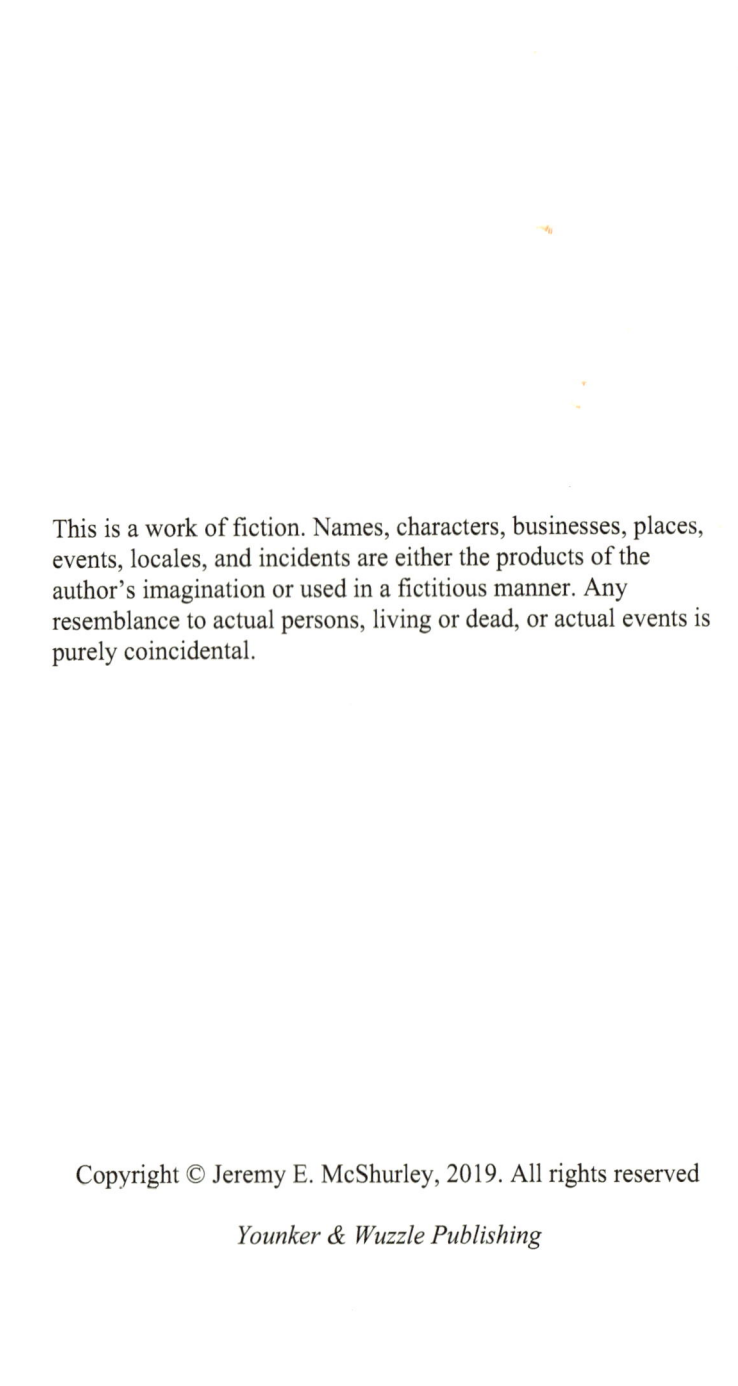

This is a work of fiction. Names, characters, businesses, places, events, locales, and incidents are either the products of the author's imagination or used in a fictitious manner. Any resemblance to actual persons, living or dead, or actual events is purely coincidental.

Copyright © Jeremy E. McShurley, 2019. All rights reserved

*Younker & Wuzzle Publishing*

Dedication

To my lady, Danielle, for who without, this book would not be possible.

## Introduction

As children we count the days until adulthood. The freedom of choice displayed by adults appears to be liberating compared to the rules and guidelines that must be followed when we are young. As we age, we realize that those rules do not vanish, but instead transform themselves into the responsibilities of being a grownup and the routine of everyday life.

We come to find that our recreation is also limited at times. Bowling lanes close, bartenders make last calls, and bank accounts run dry. Even the movies we watch and the books we read are presented in a way that takes us from Point A to Point B, reminding us of the tedium of existence.

*The Virtue of Vices* is as opportunity to break away from life's monotony and discover the world of White River City. The chapters are presented alphabetically and may be read in any desired order. There is no right or wrong way to explore the story. The only rule is that there are no rules.

This is a novel for adults. Its contents are of a mature nature and thus require a developed mind capable of interpreting the story's intricacies and subject matter. But it is also an opportunity to return to childhood, when we were inexperienced and excited to learn what the universe had to offer.

## Table of Contents

Addiction……………………..…..……………..…1

Bigotry………………..…...……………………..12

Conceit……………………..……………………24

Dependency……………………………………35

Extremism……………..…………………….46

Fixation…………………………………….56

Gambling……………………..………67

Hoarding...…..…………..……………..79

Indecency…………………………………..90

Jealousy……………………...…….………101

Lust……………………………….…..……..111

Materialism……………………………….…..122

Narcissism…………………………….....133

Obstinacy………………….……………......145

Promiscuity…………….………………..157

Rage…………………………………..169

Spite……………………………………181

Venality……………………………..……..192

Wastefulness…………………………...…..203

Zealotry…………………………….………..214

The Virtue of Vices – Jeremy McShurley

**Addiction** - *(uh-dik-shuhn)*
Inability to disengage from repetitive and/or harmful activities or stimuli

"Another."
In a hole-in-the-wall establishment on the west side of White River City, Clint obliged his customer, an off-duty officer who sat slumped on a broken stool at the end of the counter. Like so many towns and cities in the Rust Belt, White River City was a shadow of its former self. Only a couple of generations ago, a kid could graduate from high school, get a great union job in one of the local factories, start a family, and retire with pride. Today, that wasn't the case, as the factories were replaced by more and more hole-in-the-wall establishments each and every year.
"Another."
Again, Clint filled a shot glass with the bar's well vodka. Officer Grant Carroll had lost count, and as the clear liquor made its way down his throat, he entered that magical point of binge drinking, where either the burning would stop, or the vomiting would begin. He reached for his chaser, now a watered down pop, and gently sipped on it. A mixture of bile and booze met the cola halfway up his esophagus, and this time the pop won the battle of the liquids, with a light assist from gravity. Officer Carroll belched, and then exhaled the rotten stench of cheap drinks, burgers, and fries.
"Another."
"Maybe you oughta wait," Clint began.
"Another," Officer Carroll sternly banged the shot glass on the counter twice.

The call came in over the radio as Officer Carroll and his fat, piss poor excuse for a partner were only blocks away from pulling into the Princemoore University police station and clocking out for the night.

"Damnit. Just take a left here, and we can get around."

"Are you seriously suggesting that instead of heading to the scene, we head back to the station?" Officer Carroll asked his fat, piss poor excuse for a partner. He had turned on his lights but not the sirens, as he ignored his partner's advice and proceeded forward towards the University Mall.

"I'm just saying that if we hadn't hit those three red lights coming back that we'd already be in the station. And there's no way they'd let us go back out. Not this close to end of our shift."

"Well, we're not at the station, now are we?" Officer Carroll slammed on his brakes, just a few feet from a group of people who had gathered in the street. He got out and made his way towards them.

"We have a report of shots fired at the coffee shop?" he asked anyone who would listen.

The crowd agreed.

"Are there any employees here?" he continued the line of questioning.

"Yes," replied the shaky voice of a young female employee. She slowly walked towards the officer.

"Any other employees inside? Did all the customers make it out?"

"I'm not. Oh, God. I think, Jason. Oh, God, I think Jason might still be inside!"

The Virtue of Vices – Jeremy McShurley

The employee started shouting and became frantic, turning instinctively to go inside and check on her co-worker.

Officer Carroll grabbed her by the shoulders and looked directly at her. "What's your name?"

"Kelly," she gasped for breath as she began to sob with panic.

"Ok, Kelly. I need you to stay here and make sure your customers are all right. Can you do that for me?"

Kelly took a few deep breaths and turned back towards the cafe's patrons, "Alright, everyone. I'm sure the officers are going to want to ask you some questions. Could everyone please remain here until you are asked to leave?" Each sentence gave Kelly a bit more confidence, and the thoughts of her co-workers faded as her new responsibility took charge of her fear and shock.

Officer Carroll looked towards the cruiser and saw his fat, piss poor excuse for a partner still sitting inside, oblivious.

"Holy shit that felt good," Officer Carroll's fat, piss poor excuse for a partner informed him and anyone else within earshot about his most recent trip to the restroom.

"Broke the seal, huh?" Officer Carroll spun around on his seat and looked at the jukebox. The music had shut off a couple of minutes ago, and with closing time being just around the corner, people were reluctant to put their money into the machine. Officer Carroll was in no state of mind to make such calculations, and he stumbled over towards the jukebox. He leaned up against it, bending forward to get a better look at the choices. His double vision didn't help him to make a selection. He reached into his pocket and pulled out a wad of singles. After dropping them and picking them back up a couple of times, he managed to get the machine to accept a couple of the ragged bills.

Officer Carroll smiled about his victory over technology and started pressing the right arrow button on the control panel, causing the collection of CD covers to flip to each next page. Reaching the end, he began flipping the pages to the left. He then repeated the process, going through the entire catalog several times. Each time the faces of the artists became a bit blurrier, looking more and more like the witnesses he had questioned earlier that night.

In the distance, Officer Carroll could make out each unit's particular sound, as the shrieking cacophony of sirens came closer and closer. "Did you see the assailant or assailants?"

A kid wearing a hoodie and jeans answered, "I think there was only one. It all happened really quick," the kid rubbed his face with both palms.

"What about you?" Officer Carroll began to get a general assessment on what had just gone down. He started asking the different witnesses what they had seen.

"I was towards the back with some friends. Up towards the front I heard what sounded like gunshots, then some screams."

"I think, five to ten shots, maybe more."

"People started freaking out. Some ran to the kitchen, others out the emergency exit."

"The guy, he was wearing, I dunno, something like a monk's robes. I didn't see his face. It was covered."

"Made me think of church. Like Jesus on the cross, with the thorns in his head and him all looking up and stuff."

"Yeah, it was weird. It was, like, some wooden mask. But I remember those eyes. Piercing, cold blue eyes."

Even this late at night the west side bar had a decent crowd. It was slower than normal, but nothing the bartenders would want to complain about. The clicks and clacks of pool games constantly came from one darkened corner. On the other side, the cackles and giggles of a bachelorette party drew occasional attention from the rest of the barflies. A group of older bikers threw down their last few dollars as they competed against one another at darts along the back wall.

"You gonna play something, boss?" asked a tall gentleman wearing cowboy boots and the ensemble to match

"Hmm? Yeah, there's just so many to pick," Officer Carroll noted, coming back to reality.

"I'll pick some for ya," offered the cowboy.

"Sure. Sounds good," Officer Carroll turned to return to his seat, but lost his balance and started to fall to his knees.

The cowboy quickly grabbed him by the waist until he had regained his balance. "You gonna be alright there, boss?"

"Yeah. Long day," Officer Carroll gently pulled himself up to his feet and nodded to his human walking stick.

The cowboy shook his head and watched as Officer Carroll zigzagged his way back to his seat and plopped down next to an overweight gentleman wearing black slacks and a white wife-beater. He then used up Officer Carroll's credits and added a few of his own. The sounds of music again filled the air of the saloon, as an old country ballad summoned a few lovers, both old and new, to the dance floor.

"You wanna switch to coffee?" Clint asked.

The two officers cautiously entered the coffee shop with guns drawn and reactions set to their highest levels. They quickly scanned the room. The entrance was wide, about twelve by four feet. Moving forward, one would have to either take a couple of steps or the nearby ramp to ascend to the front counter. The counter area had all the standard coffee shop accoutrements, and a pair of metal swinging doors led to what only could be assumed to be the kitchen and perhaps offices.

To the right of the entrance was a doorway with a sign overhead that read "General Store". This part of the cafe was one of White River City's oldest buildings. While the city's downtown had originated on the west side, there had been plenty of space on the east side of the White River for early settlers to unload their wagons. Roth's General Store was the result of one of those settler's endeavors. When the Princemoore family purchased the land to build the college that would eventually become Princemoore University, Roth's General Store was kept intact as an historical landmark. Even when the renovations of the 1970s built the University Mall, Roth's old building remained. Today, students used the space to sell their artwork, freecycle, or barter for goods and services the old fashion way.

On the other side of the entrance was the main seating. Originally this area was designed with matching booths and chairs, lined up either against the wall or set spaced out in the center of the room.

The Virtue of Vices – Jeremy McShurley

But the Blizzard of '78 caused the roof to collapse, destroying most of that side's interior as well. Loyal coffee drinkers and scone eaters pitched in with the cleanup and had the roof fixed within a few days. To repair the interior, they gathered a motley crew of furniture just to fill space until a new set could be ordered. The owners liked the new look so much they kept it. From that time on, old couches and chairs were donated to incoming freshman, replaced by the loveseats and end tables of graduating seniors.

Clint's suggestion of coffee was ignored and instead Grant's fat, piss poor excuse for a partner clinked his bottle against Officer Carroll's longneck, "Cheers."
"What are we cheering?" Officer Carroll asked.
"Not getting coffee at one in the morning. What? Too soon?"
"I've never seen anything like that. Not in all my time on the force," Officer Carroll reflected. He downed his bottle of beer, and then pointed to it indicating he wanted another.
"Gonna be last call here pretty soon," Clint told Officer Carroll, subtly trying to let him know he'd probably had enough. Clint was in a particularly precarious position. As a bartender, he had a duty not to over serve his customers, including policemen. But as a citizen he knew it was good to have a couple of cops on your side.
"Is it? Wow, that went fast, "Officer Carroll noted. "Better make it two. And get this asshole a couple as well," he said, pointing to his fat, piss poor excuse for a partner.
"You got a ride home, Grant?" Clint had been serving Grant Carroll drinks for many years

now. This was by far the most wasted he'd ever seen him, even on his 21st eleven years ago. He knew that Grant and his wife had been fighting lately, but this was more than a steam-blowing bender.

"I'll just walk. I'm not that far," he slurred, again cheersing his fat, piss poor excuse for a partner. "Here's to, what'd you say? 'Not getting coffee at one in the morning.'"

"Almost made it," pointed out the fat, piss poor excuse for a partner as he laboriously bent over to check the logo on the apron. Sure enough, it matched the design above the front door, a giant beanstalk with different types of coffee mugs hanging from the branches. The employee was a young male, barely old enough to grow stubble. His head was pointed towards the double metal doors only a couple of feet away, most likely the direction he was heading.

Officer Carroll wondered if this might be Jason. He was dead; a shotgun wound to the back had most likely killed him instantly. There were a couple of bloody footprints on his shirt that lead towards the double doors, indicating he may have been trampled as well. Officer Carroll tried to imagine the chaos; gunshots ringing out, people yelling and running in every direction. He hoped this would be the only corpse they found. He knew in his heart he was wrong.

"Register doesn't look touched," Officer Carroll's fat, piss poor excuse for a partner mentioned as he shoved a raspberry and cream cheese pastry into his mouth.

"Great detective work," he snidely replied as he crept towards the General Store. An elderly black gentleman, wearing one of those ugly brown suits that only look good on elderly gentlemen lay in a pool of his own blood. Officer Carroll could swear that the look on his face was not that of shock or pain, but perhaps relief. In addition to the doorway from the coffee shop, the General Store still maintained its original entrance. He prayed everyone else who had been in the room had made it out.

    A crash from behind him sent Officer Carroll spinning around with his weapon pointed towards the unknown assailant. Instead, he saw his fat, piss poor excuse for a partner hovering over a broken jar of cookies.

    "It was already like that," he assured Officer Carroll, mouth stuffed full of chocolate chips and baked cookie dough.

    From his vantage point, Officer Carroll could see a pair of legs sticking out from around the corner in the main dining area. As he entered the room he found more victims. Below him laid another young kid, this one wearing jeans and a windbreaker, an empty coffee mug nearby. Maybe he was sobering up from partying all night. Maybe he was pulling an all-nighter. Regardless, he had no idea he had just finished his last cup o' joe.

    On a loveseat to the right appeared to be two college students. The female, body leaning towards the left, had short brown hair and wore a blouse that was probably pink, but was now saturated in blood. The male's body was propped up to the right side of the loveseat, chest blown open. His jet-black hair was pulled back into a ponytail, and his grey eyes now stared into the face of Thanatos. Officer Carroll noticed their hands on the cushion; fingers just centimeters away from touching as though their ghosts had tried to move their bodies in one last desperate attempt to hold hands.

Officer Carroll completed the sweep of the room. There were seven victims in total so far. It occurred to him that some people might have found a place to hide in the kitchen. He grabbed his fat, piss poor excuse for a partner and the two entered through the swinging metal doors. First, they checked the walk-in coolers to no avail. Then the two officers looked in the dry storage area before moving towards the offices that they also found empty. Down the hall they heard a slight banging coming from the back door and took cover as best they could before it swung open.

"Put your weapons down, officers," ordered a slightly raspy voice. Detective Tranche walked in and began to survey the area.

Officer Carroll and his fat, piss poor excuse for a partner complied with the detective.

"There's a few victims in the front," Officer Carroll began.

"That's alright, boys. We can take it from here. Great work, thanks for your help." Detective Tranche had glanced into the office before mumbling something into his radio and heading towards the front of house.

Officer Carroll shrugged and started heading back to his vehicle. The White River City Police Department was here. There was no point in sticking around. Technically, the University Mall was off campus and therefore under WRCPD jurisdiction. When it came to smaller crimes, like underage drinking or public intox, the two departments worked well together. In larger cases such as this, there was no way WRCPD was going to let the campus police handle the investigation.

The two campus police officers exited the back door. Officer Carroll's adrenaline level had finally started to drop. He could see the flashing lights of emergency vehicles and police cars filtering down the nearby alleyway. The sirens reverberated down as well, bouncing off the walls between the different buildings. He could see the look on every face in the coffee shop. He could visualize the assailant pulling the trigger over and over again, until the rooms were silent. Officer Carroll bent over, put his hands on his knees, and emptied his entire stomach onto the pavement.

"Guess we better get you something in that gut of yours. I'll buy the first round."

Clint and Officer Carroll's fat, piss poor excuse for a partner heaved Grant's limp body onto one of the pool tables. Clint stuffed a jacket under his head and threw a sweatshirt over his body as best he could.

"I've never seen Grant so drunk he couldn't even walk home. What happened tonight?"

Officer Carroll's fat, piss poor excuse for a partner walked up to the bar, reached over the counter and grabbed a bottle of whatever. He poured two shots, offered one to Clint and recounted the night's events from the coffee shop.

"Damn, man. That's fucked up, like something outta a movie," Clint held the bottle tilted downward, letting every last drop hit the glass. He set the empty bottle down. "I can't even imagine what that must have been like. You sure as hell handled it better than Grant." Clint wished he could take those words back as he noticed a fresh bottle had just been placed on the counter.

"Another."

**Bigotry** - *(big-uh-tree)*
Inclination to show disdain for those who share opposite or opposing views than oneself

      Although the season of the year had recently moved from summer into autumn, a warm southern breeze still permeated the air. Laurie Kozlowski sat in the passenger's seat of her father's car, breathing in the fresh smells that blew through the open windows. Classes were out for the day as the annual parent/teacher conferences were being held this weekend. Her father, Paul, would be meeting with her middle school's teachers tomorrow and the two had decided to take advantage of the break by spending the day together. Laurie began to fidget with the radio dial as she waited for her father to come out of the dollar store.
      *"Welcome back to the 24-hour Marathon of* The Leon Joneway Show; *this is your host, Leon Joneway. This hour's broadcast is brought to you by Athena's Pizzeria. 'The highest quality ingredients for the lowest prices... Athena's Pizzeria. It's the wise choice.' And as we move into the noon hour of our marathon, I must admit that I've been enjoying a couple of slices from Athena's. How about you, Gordy?"*
      *"Oh yeah. It's the best."*
      *"I couldn't agree more. Now, personally, I'm partial to a good ole slice of pepperoni. I tell ya, it's hard to go wrong with pepperoni. What about you, Gordy?"*
      *"I'm a fan of green peppers, mushrooms, onions, and olives."*
      *"Well, you better let me know if there's any mushrooms on my slice. That'd send me on a little*

*trip to the hospital, and you'd be doing the rest of the show without me."*

Laurie's stomach began to rumble at the talk of food. Although she'd love to suggest Athena's for lunch her father had already decided on going to Pattywack's, an Irish bar and grill chain that was located on Broad Street, known more colloquially as "The Strip." She looked into the window of the dollar store and saw her father standing in line at the register.

*"Now, normally we'd be going off the air in an hour, but this is no normal day. You think you've got another eighteen hours in you, Gordy?"*

*"You know it, Leon."*

*"I know I'll be able to stay awake the whole time, but I sure hope I don't lose my voice. That's why I'm fully stocked up on water. 'Lethe Bottled Water... forget about your thirst...with Lethe'. We have some great guests joining us here in the studio as we discuss gun rights. Terry Alcorn is from* Citizens for the Second Amendment. *Welcome."*

*"Thanks for having me, Leon."*

*"And we also have Alicia Newsome. Alicia is a gun control activist from the non-for profit,* Parents of Fallen Children."

*"Thank you, Leon, although we prefer the term 'gun reform' rather than 'gun control.' It's a misconception that organizations such as ours want to dismantle the Second Amendment. We support the Bill of Rights as much as any other American. But just like the Supreme Court has made modifications to the interpretation of the First Amendment over the years, we believe the Second Amendment needs to be interpreted in a way that falls in line with today's realities. And the reality is that we're not just firing muskets anymore."*

*"If I might jump in here, Leon. What Alicia and her group of gun grabbers is proposing is nothing more than the slippery slope of Fascism. Hitler, Stalin, Mao; all those dictators took the guns and look at where that got those countries. And we're not just going to sit back and let you and your leftist friends take away the freedoms our soldiers died protecting!"*

*"Now wait just one moment! I'm offended that you would put me and the organization I represent into the same category as those vile individuals. Children are dying in the streets, some as young as two years old. Gun violence is a plague on our inner cities, and you and your group just want to turn a blind eye!"*

*"Well maybe if more of our citizens were better armed they could better defend themselves against those thugs."*

Laurie looked up and noticed her father leaving the store, both hands clutching several plastic bags filled with an assortment of goodies. She got out of her seat and went to the other side of the car to open the back door.

"Thanks," said Paul as he tossed his purchases into the back. He then sat down in the driver's seat as Laurie returned to the front. "Well, you and the girls should be fully stocked for tonight's slumber party. I got you chips, cookies, popcorn, pop, candy, the works."

"I saw. It looks like you got us enough for a week of slumber parties," Laurie graciously smiled.

"You can never have enough treats. And you're sure you'll be alright with me playing cards tonight?" Paul had started the car and began driving away from the parking lot.

"Yes, gosh. You act like I haven't been babysitting for the last year or something," Laurie shook her head, frustrated at her father's lack of confidence.

The argument from the radio continued to get louder, and Paul turned his attention to the show. "What the hell are you listening to?"

"*The Leon Joneway Show,*" Laurie casually answered.

"Leon Joneway! That right-wing nutjob?" Paul went to change the channel but Laurie put her hand over the knob.

"What's wrong with a little news?" she asked as both pulled their hands away and Paul returned his attention to the road.

"It's not news, Laurie, it's a bunch of trash. 'Blah blah blah, your ideas are stupid. Blah blah blah, my ideas are good'." he said in a mocking tone.

"My teachers have been saying we need to spend less time online and more time listening to traditional broadcasts," Laurie interjected. "He's doing a twenty-four hour marathon today, and I thought it'd be a good idea to see what's going on in the world."

"Then you'll have plenty of time to listen later tonight with your friends." Paul pressed the memory button for his favorite station. The sound of angry pundits was quickly replaced by the music from Paul's childhood. "See, that's better."

Paul started singing along to one of his favorite songs as the two made their way towards Pattywack's. Laurie stared out the open window in silence, trying to ignore her father's tone-deaf performance. As the song ended, Paul turned down the volume.

"You know, when I was your age, I never listened to the news. I just wanted to shoot hoops and play video games. You must get that from your mother. How is she, by the way?"

"She's fine."

"How about your step-dad?"

"He's fine, too," Laurie continued to pout.

"You mad at me?" Paul asked in a pitiful tone.

Laurie refused to answer, continuing with the silent treatment.

Paul sighed, "I think it's great you're interested in that sort of thing. But Leon Joneway? Seriously? That guy is the worst of the worst. He puts two people against one another, knowing full well they're going to get into a shouting match. Then, he always ends up siding with the conservative and tries to make the liberal look like a fool. He's not trying to do the news; he's just trying to get ratings. I don't know how you can put up with that guy."

"Just because you disagree with someone doesn't mean you shouldn't listen. Maybe you should have done that with Mom," Laurie finished with the last part under her breath.

Paul started to open his mouth to respond but instead snapped it shut and pretended not to hear. His parents had divorced as well, and he knew how hard it was for a child in that situation. He and Laurie's mother had married just after high school. But as they grew into adulthood they also grew apart. Over time their marriage became more and more strained, and even the birth of their child couldn't reconcile their differences. While their relationship didn't end up working out, he swore that wouldn't happen with Laurie.

## The Virtue of Vices – Jeremy McShurley

Paul's station had gone to commercial, and he started going through his saved channels. He stopped when he heard the familiar and popular tune of Laurie's favorite boy band, Addled Essence. After suffering through a couple of bars of her father butchering the lyrics, Laurie's scowl began to transform into a reluctant smile. The chorus kicked in and they both turned towards one another singing in unison.

"'Cuz you're so sweet, sweet, sweet and so neat, neat, neat. I just want to fall and worship at your feet. You're so hot, hot, hot, and I'm not, not, not. But I gotta crush that ain't never, ever gonna stop'." Laurie cranked the volume to full blast as the two belted out tunes and swerved through the lunch-hour traffic of The Strip.

Brandie ducked under the heat lamps of the expo line and leaned as far into the Pattywack's kitchen as possible. "Hey. How much longer on table 19?"

"About five minutes," responded one of the line cooks.

"That's what you said five minutes ago," she called back, obviously frustrated.

Another cook chimed in, "Oh, gee, I'm sorry. I guess no one told you that we get really busy at lunch." The kitchen staff laughed at the comment as they worked to prepare meals for a nearly full restaurant.

"Assholes." Brandie pulled her head back and turned to look around for a manager. Noticing the kitchen manager standing by the to go counter, she hastily made her way over to him.

"Hey, Don. I've been waiting for almost twenty minutes for some motz sticks and onion rings. Is that pretty normal?" Brandie hadn't been working for Pattywack's very long, but she was a veteran of the food service industry. She knew that fried food normally took the least amount of time to prepare and in the back of her mind she wondered if she might be going through a bit of a hazing period with the kitchen staff.

"No, not usually. But I guess a few schools in the area are having parent/teacher conferences, so we're a little busier than normal. You want me to say something?"

"Nah, just checking. I'm still learning the ropes a bit, I guess," Brandie shrugged. She knew that sending a manager to the line would only further antagonize the cooks.

Don nodded and gently patted her on the shoulder. "You're doing a great job. But remember, there's no 'I' in 'TEAM'," he said, pulling a phrase from his recent management seminar. "And what does 'TEAM' stand for?"

Brandie responded a line from her orientation from a few weeks ago, "'Thoughtful Enthusiastic Appreciative Motivated'."

"That's the spirit," Don said with a smile and a thumbs up. "What table is waiting?"

"Nineteen," she explained.

"If I see that food up, I'll run it out there for ya, deal?" he promised.

"Thanks, Don," Brandie said, feeling somewhat less stressed.

Don walked to the side door to hold it open for some exiting patrons, "Thanks for coming to Pattywack's. 'Have a Lucky Day.'"

Brandie walked back to the expo line to look for her food but to no avail. For a moment she caught the look of one of the cooks. "Guess the new girl's being a bitch again, huh?" she said jokingly.

The cook smiled, "You're cool. Sorry, my baskets have been full since we opened. I'll give you a shout soon as it comes up. Brandie, right?"

"Yeah," she confirmed. "Thanks."

Over her years in food service, she had worked in both the kitchen and on the dining room floor. Normally she wasn't so impatient with the kitchen staff, as she had been in their shoes before. But her husband's chronic unemployment and their overall financial situation had left her more tense than usual. Plus, the lack of sleep from working two jobs only added to her anxiety. Glancing one last time at the expo window, she gulped down a bit of soda then made her way back towards the front-of-house.

The restaurant looked even busier since she had last been on the floor only minutes ago. But, she had hired in just as the summer was ending and things always picked up at the beginning of fall. Not only that, with the thousands of students returning to town for classes at nearby Princemoore University, the population of White River City expanded as it did every year at this time. Standing by the door into the back-of-house she scanned her tables from afar. Brandie tried to note if any of her guests looked like they needed anything. Mostly, she was trying to avoid table 19 until their food was done. She felt a touch on her arm and turned to face one of the hostesses.

"Can you pick up table 31? I know it's not your section but Bart's really backed up," the hostess pleaded.

"Sure," Brandie heaved a sigh of relief, knowing that table 31 was on the other side of the restaurant, away from her other guests. It would also keep them from asking her about their food. She walked by the Pattywack's logo that was displayed in the middle of the wall, a cheery, flush-cheeked leprechaun standing next to a pot with the restaurant's name streaming out of it in rainbow colors. Tradition held that each server should touch the leprechaun's belly for luck before greeting a new table. Considering the day she was having, Brandie decided to give the company mascot a couple of pats this time.

Her new table was an adult male and a young girl who appeared to be in her teens. The guy was wearing blue jeans, a wrinkled t-shirt, and a baseball cap. The girl was wearing a flowery sundress, and her hair was pulled back into a ponytail. Both the gentleman and girl had light brown hair and hazel eyes. Brandie also noted they shared similar facial features, and she assumed they must be father and daughter.

"Hi, welcome to Pattywack's. My name's Brandie and I'll be your server." She suddenly remembered her boss mentioning the parent/teacher conferences. "Are we out of school today?" she asked, looking at the young girl.

"Yes. You guys are busy," noted the young girl.

"You ain't lying there," Brandie agreed. "So, it might take a little longer than normal. Hope you're not in a hurry."

The gentleman laughed, "Anyone who goes to a sit down restaurant on a Friday at lunch and expects fast food is an idiot."

Brandie wanted to agree but the job required her to take a more diplomatic tone. "We try to get our food out as quickly as possible to all our guests."

## The Virtue of Vices – Jeremy McShurley

The girl pointed her thumb towards Brandie and winked at the gentleman, "She's good."

Brandie smiled at the compliment, "So, can I start you off with a drink or appetizer?"

At that point, the gentleman's phone began to vibrate on the table and he quickly picked it up. "Yeah, hey, hold on, I'm having lunch… what? No, I said put 200 on the Stallions and three on the Leopards. Yes, yes I did. Hold on." The gentleman put his hand over the phone and turned to the young girl.

"Hey, Laurie, honey. I gotta go take care of some business. Why don't you go ahead and order some food and I'll be back as soon as I can."

"Sure," Laurie agreed as her father picked up his conversation and made his way out the side door of the building.

"Do you want me to come back in a minute?" Brandie asked Laurie.

"No. He does this all the time," she replied in a dour voice.

Another server rushed up to Brandie. "Uh, nineteen needs to see you."

She cursed under her breath. "Do they still not have their apps?"

"No, they got those. They're just ready to order," the other server reassured her.

"Whew. Ok, thanks." Brandie turned back to the little girl. "Laurie, was it?"

"Yeah," she said as she flipped back and forth between the pages of her menu.

"I'm gonna give you a few minutes to think about your order, ok? Did you want a drink?"

"I'm ok with water." Laurie closed the menu and began to play with the condiment tray.

"You sure? How about a chocolate shake? On the house," Brandie prompted with a slight tilt of her head.

Laurie's eyes lit up at the sound of her offer. "Yeah. With extra cherries?"

Brandie nodded and wrote down the order out of habit. "You got it."

After taking the order from table 19 and checking on her other guests she went to the dessert station to make Laurie's milkshake. She then grabbed a small ramekin and filled it with maraschino cherries. Laurie was still sitting alone when Brandie returned to their booth.

"Dad not back yet?" she asked as she set down the milkshake and cherries.

"Nope," Laurie responded. She had dumped out a couple of sugar packets onto the table and was tracing through the crystals with her fingernail.

"You know, he works that hard because he loves you," Brandie explained, trying to comfort Laurie.

"He's not working. He's gambling. Sounded like football," Laurie said as she blew the pile of sugar off the table.

Hearing this enraged Brandie to no end. Her eyes began to well with tears as she plopped down across the table from Laurie and took her hands, "Oh my God. Do you need me to call someone? Social services? A relative?"

Laurie was caught off guard by the sudden sentiment and had to choke back a lump in her throat. "I'm fine. I live with my mom. I just get to see Dad mostly on the weekends. He does what he can. He's just been in a bit of a slump lately. It was really nice of you to offer."

Laurie started sucking down her milkshake, and then stopped suddenly and with wide-open eyes stated, "Brain freeze!"

Brandie could only laugh at the situation and Laurie chuckled along with her. Wiping a bit of tears from the corner of her eyes she stood back up and pulled out her notebook. "Did you decide on any food yet?"

"Um, sure. Let's do the Dublin Sampler Platter with extra ranch," Laurie said, pointing at the picture in the menu.

"You got it," Brandie wrote down the order.

"And if my dad's not back when it gets here, maybe you can help me eat it," Laurie offered with an ear-to-ear grin.

Brandie smiled back, "We'll see. Hey, why don't you come with me for a second?" Brandie extended her hand and Laurie took it and followed her to the Pattywack's logo.

"This here is Mickey McMickerton," Brandie explained to Laurie. "At least, that's what everyone around here calls him. Why don't you give him a couple of pats on the belly."

"For what?" Laurie asked while still following through with Brandie's request.

"For luck."

**Conceit** - *(kuhn-seet)*
Feelings of superiority about one's capabilities, significance, or position

Other than the business district and a few scattered small stores, the Downtown area of White River City was a financial wasteland. The blight and decay stemming from the west side's manufacturing decline spread eastward until it stopped at the White River and the developments of the Princemoore family on the other side. There was, however, a small strip of businesses on Main Street that still survived, mostly due to the patronage of students from Princemoore University. For the most part, bars, art shops, and a couple of restaurants comprised central Main Street. At the center of the activity was a club called Holidaze, one of only a few live music venues in the city.

During the Counterculture Revolution of the 1960's, Holidaze was known as Whispering Willie's, named after its proprietor "Whispering" Willie Jacoby. Willie was a veteran of the Korean War and had been wounded by shrapnel from a landmine. The explosion damaged his vocal chords, and from that time he was never able to speak above a whisper. Upon his return home he fell in with the beatnik crowd. Years later Willie grew out his beard and hair and joined the ranks of the hippies. Using up most of his inheritance, he purchased a three-story former department store from the 40s, and turned it into an urban commune for artists, drifters, and other revolutionaries.

Whispering Willie's became a hub of activity, especially for Princemoore University's students. On the top floor were numerous bunk beds, cots, hammocks, and sleeping bags for anyone who needed a place to crash. The second floor was a studio for the most part, where painters and poets shared their love for the arts and love with one another. Downstairs is where most of the musicians gathered, hosting open mic nights, holding drum circles, and throwing a few concerts now and again. As for the basement, it was off limits to most of the patrons, and it was rumored that several anti-government groups had used the space to plan their attacks and protests.

Around the same time, Raymond Princemoore was attempting to revitalize Downtown, as most of its inhabitants and businesses had either moved to the suburban town of Santa Mesa or across the river to be closer to the university and the East Bank District. Raymond wanted to convert Willie's building into luxury apartments, but no matter the amount of money offered, Willie refused to sell. Then, in the dead of night during the middle of winter, the police and FBI raided the commune on the grounds that minors were being held against their will. Although no one younger than sixteen was inside and child endangerment charges were never filed, the authorities did find enough drugs on the premises to arrest Willie.

As Willie sat in a jail cell, Raymond Princemoore and his cadre of lawyers worked behind the scenes to acquire the building. The artists who lived there did their best to keep the place running, but Willie was the heart and soul of the operation. Not only that, several undercover Feds infiltrated the group. They stirred up animosity between the commune's members, sending over half their numbers to seek out greener pastures. By the time Willie was released, there were only fifteen residents left. And by then it was too late for him to restore his haven to its former glory. The banks repossessed the property and quickly sold it to Raymond's businesses.

    The remaining members of the commune hunkered down as best they could. They sealed themselves on the top floor with enough food and water to last several months. Every night they would move up to the roof and sing songs about peace, love, and harmony for your fellow man. The protest actually drew some national headlines for a while, but after the first month, most of the city simply saw them as a nuisance. As the food ran low, the last of the commune's members took up the offer to turn themselves in for lesser charges. In one final act of defiance, Willie silently threw himself from the top of the building. There was a note pinned to his shirt that read, *You can take this building but you'll never take its spirit! - Willie.* Some say his ghost still roams the top floor to this day.

    Willie's suicide and the accompanying bad press spooked most of the investors and potential renters. The building ended up sitting vacant for nearly twenty years before anyone showed any interest in using it again. A small group of Princemoore University students teamed up with a local musician named Admiral Davidson and purchased the building for pennies on the dollar. Playing off the building's background and supposed haunting, it was opened again as The Coven and catered to the local Goth scene of the time. As Goth died out in popularity, The Coven adapted to the growing electronic rave culture. But bad management and multiple drug raids saw the ownership shift several times through the early 21st century.

    In the mid-2000s the new owners changed both the name and appearance to its current form. Rather than relying on local bands to fill the lineups, they utilized the Internet to bring in out of town acts and their loyal fan bases. And instead of being genre specific like The Coven, Holidaze branched out to encompass the entire music scene; from rock to rap to metal to country. The second floor was converted into a recording studio while the third provided traveling acts a place to sleep for the night. The venue also served as a springboard for local acts onto the regional and even national stage. Tonight, Caleb Brown and The Skunk Munkies were making their triumphant return to the club that had started their successful career.

    Over the years the owners had developed an efficient and successful system. The doors opened at six, and the music began with either karaoke or open mic. Holidaze had a fully stocked bar and a kitchen that slung baskets of greasy fried food to hungry guests. At eight o'clock a local band would open the show, followed by a bigger regional act in the nine o'clock hour. Brent Carmichael was currently running the soundboard for that regional act; a mariachi-ska band named Rusty Trombone and the Dirty Sanchezes.

    Brent's employment at Holidaze had come by complete accident. Just over a year ago a fight had broken out during a death metal concert. As the melee escalated the bouncers quickly became overwhelmed, and several of the staff had to come to their assistance. Brent had managed to back away from the scuffle and was standing next to the sound booth when the sound guy decided he needed to jump in as well. He looked at Brent as said, "You know how to run this thing?"

    Brent shook his head.

"It's easy," the sound guy said pointing to the board. "Just push the slider up to make things louder, pull it down to make it softer. All the instruments are labeled at the bottom. Got it?"

Brent shrugged his shoulders, downed his whiskey and cola and jumped up into the booth. He put on the headphones and scanned over the soundboard's controls. A lot of the terms didn't make sense, but he did understand things like "High", "Mid", and "Low". As the lead guitarist went into his solo, Brent pushed the instrument's volume up a couple of notches. As it ended, he brought it back down to its original level. While not technically proficient with this hardware, Brent was a huge fan of music in general, and he spent a good deal of his spare time hanging out at Holidaze. He started to fiddle with the equalization of each instrument, adjusting their tones to his preferred specifications. Brent became lost in the moment and didn't even notice that the fight had been broken up or that the sound guy was standing behind him.

The band ended their set to a round of screams, shouts, and applause. Brent took off the headphones and turned around to be startled by the sight of the sound guy.

"Damn, man. For not knowing what the fuck you're doing you sure have a knack for this. Why don't you come back tomorrow around two and I'll show you a few more tricks." Those tricks turned into a part-time gig, and when Brent's mentor got a job on the west coast, he ended up taking over the position full time.

Rusty Trombone and the Dirty Sanchezes consisted of a guitarist/lead singer, a bassist, a drummer, trumpet, trombone, and violin players, and a female backup singer who also played occasional

The Virtue of Vices – Jeremy McShurley

percussion instruments. Brent had been the one to discover them online and then bring them to the attention of the booking manager. He loved how they fused the upbeat rhythms of ska with the traditional chord structure of Mexican folk music. Brent knew their songs very well and had no problem setting their levels to give the crowd the perfect mix.

Out of the corner of his eye, Brent saw some kid peering over the top of the sound booth wall. He removed his headphones and leaned towards him.

"Hey, man," the kid yelled. "You gotta crank that bass, bitch. Crank it!"

Brent smirked at him with disdain and put his headphones back on. He couldn't understand why everyone wanted to "crank that bass." This wasn't dance music or some rap act that required more low end. The focus right now should be on the melody and the intricate balance between the brass and vocals. Brent might not have studied music engineering at school, but he knew full well what he was doing. As he looked over at the set list for the next act, his mind drifted back to his earlier encounter with Caleb Brown and The Skunk Munkies.

The band had rolled into town late Thursday night. Their tour bus and Caleb's RV took up several parking spaces in the lot behind Holidaze, a move not appreciated by a couple of the local business owners. But their presence was certain to bring in plenty of fans from miles around, and the Downtown area would be happy to see those extra dollars spent. Besides that, most of the owners had known about Caleb since he was a young man. They would have been thrilled for him to grace their establishment with his presence.

Brent usually showed up to Holidaze around noon. The management staff liked to have daily meetings, as coordinating multiple acts on an almost nightly basis was an intricate affair. There were certain misconceptions about the music industry, especially among concertgoers. Most fans weren't privy to the behind the scenes machinations that allowed the engines to keep the music running. Booking had to create a schedule, promotions had to hang up fliers and post on social media, and the bar and kitchen needed to keep the inventory stocked. And the production team needed to be aware of any artist riders so they could prepare appropriate hospitality and technical specifications. The staff put in ten to fourteen hours a day, but the end results were what made Holidaze so popular with the clientele.

Following the meeting, Brent started going through his routine; checking the inventory, testing equipment, and running cables to the appropriate locations. He preferred working with professionals like Caleb's band. Most of the smaller acts didn't show up until just before the show, sometimes loading in just before their set was to start. With the smaller acts, there were only a few minutes to perform a sound check, and most of the adjustments were done during the show. But acts like the Skunk Munkies usually set their levels hours in advance to maximize performance time.

The drummer and bassist were the first to show up. Brent introduced himself then pointed them in the direction of the stage manager who gave them a small tour and set them up backstage. Brent waited patiently for over an hour before he began to wonder when the rest of the band would come into the venue.

# The Virtue of Vices – Jeremy McShurley

He walked backstage and then down the stairs that led to the green room. "You know where everyone's at?" he asked.

The bassist was running through scales while the drummer chatted on his phone.

"Guys. We were supposed to get started about fifteen minutes ago. Everything cool?"

"Yeah, man. He's always late," the bassist responded, still practicing.

No one in the band, other than Caleb, went by their real names. The bassist was Captain Funk Munkie and the drummer was known as Tom-Tom Macaque. The band's main guitarist called himself Howler Munkie. Caleb was the lead singer, but he also played guitar and keyboards depending on the song.

"Any idea how long?" Brent questioned as his frustration level started to grow. He had heard through the grapevine that the band was a little difficult to work with, but he didn't want to get off on the wrong foot.

Captain Funk Munkie stopped playing and finally looked up. "Caleb said he was tryin' to score a bag. Said he had some connects in town. You find us some dope, and we can get this show on the road."

Brent didn't have time for this. He had a reputation to maintain, and he wasn't going to let a bunch of potheads throw him off schedule. He marched up the stairs, then out the back door of the load-in area. In the far corner of the parking lot, he saw the tour bus and RV parked parallel to one another. Brent quickly walked across the lot and went to the side of the RV. He pulled on the handle, but it appeared to be locked, so he banged several times on the door.

"Caleb!" he shouted. "Come on. Sound check. Let's move."

According to protocol, Brent should have informed either the stage or production manager about the delay. But Brent didn't usually play by the rules. Rules and guidelines were for people who needed constant attention. Most of the people in the world just stood around until told what to do, but Brent, however, took life by the horns. He hadn't always been that way. When he was younger, he always behaved around authority figures. He accepted what he was told and never asked questions. But over the years he saw politicians get away with lying on a daily basis. Corporate executives stole billions and only received a slap on the wrist, while priests molested innocent children. Instead of serving life in prison, they were shuffled around and given free reign to defile the next unsuspecting victim. Brent had learned that true happiness came from living your life they way you see fit.

"Caleb," Brent began a second round of banging. "I know you're in there. Time to be a big boy and come do your job."

A middle-aged guy with thinning slicked back hair, a beer gut, and expensive sunglasses came around from the front of the RV. "What the fuck is going on here?" he yelled.

"I'm trying to get a sound check going," Brent explained.

"Who the fuck are you?" asked the man in expensive glasses.

"Um, the sound guy. Who the fuck are you?" Brent retorted.

"Randy. I'm the band's manager. And it looks like you're about to become the ex-sound guy," Randy informed Brent as he got up in his face.

## The Virtue of Vices – Jeremy McShurley

The door to the RV opened up and Caleb leaned out. He was wearing nothing but black skinny jeans and a pair of cheap sandals. Around his neck was a talisman in the shape of a dream catcher with two blue feathers hanging down. His wavy hair was a dark brown color, and it came down just past his ears. Wafting outside with Caleb was the skunky stench of incense and marijuana.

"What gives, man? I'm trying to meditate," Caleb explained. He stepped down the steps of the RV and squinted in the sun, his bloodshot eyes trying to focus in on the commotion.

"Sorry, Caleb. I was just about to pummel some piece of shit into the ground," Randy said as he grabbed Brent's arm and wound up for a punch.

"Go ahead. Try finding somebody to run the board better than me," Brent dared the manager, lifting his head in defiance.

Randy lowered his punching arm and gave Brent a slight shove with the other. "I ain't got time for this," he said waving his arm in disgust. Randy then turned around and headed back towards the tour bus.

Caleb turned to face Brent. "Let's just be a couple of Buddhas, man," he said, touching his thumbs together with his index fingers while extending the others.

"Your manager's a dick," Brent pronounced as he looked down at the time on his phone.

"His job is to keep us safe. Everything has its place in the world. The tree provides shelter for the bird. The bird provides sustenance for the cat. The cat provides companionship to the human. And I provide the music that will one day bring peace on earth, and goodwill to all of mankind," Caleb professed as he stared at some point just above Brent's head.

"And I provide the hundreds of watts that your fans need to hear you play," Brent stated, trying his best to imitate Caleb's soft and ethereal sounding voice.

Caleb smiled. "You get it, man, you get it. Let me just, find my chi, and we'll be right in. Cool?" he requested.

"Yeah, sure. But, we don't have all day. Your opener is getting here about five," Brent informed Caleb. "Cool?"

Caleb placed his hands into a prayer position and slightly bowed. "Namaste."

The rest of the band eventually came into the venue. A small crew of roadies hauled their gear onto the stage while the band had a few drinks at the bar with the management team. Once the equipment was set up, Brent did a little grip work and returned to the booth. The check went smoothly for the most part. Tom-Tom had to replace the head on one of his drums. And Howler Munkie kicked his effects pedals around a couple of times, displeased by the monitor mix. But Brent's final adjustments and Caleb's soothing words finally calmed Howler down.

As the Skunk Munkies were just about to head off stage, Caleb called them back. They returned to their spots and took up their instruments.

"This one's for my man, Brent," Caleb announced pointing towards the sound booth. He picked up his guitar from off its stand. "It's called 'The Cycle.' One, two, three, four…"

The Virtue of Vices – Jeremy McShurley

**Dependency** - *(dih-pen-duhn-see)*
The reliance on something or someone else for protection or survival

     Brandie's hands nervously clutched the steering wheel at the 10-and-2 position. Her eyes darted back and forth from the rear view mirror to the side mirror, to the road, then back in habitual fashion. Anytime she saw headlights, either behind or in front of her, she would check her dashboard to make certain she was following the speed limit. She cursed herself for succumbing to peer pressure. Normally, Brandie would never be in this position, wondering if she was over the legal limit. But tonight had been a special night for her. For the first time since she began working at Pattywack's some of her co-workers had invited her out for post-shift drinks.

     She had been working in the foodservice industry since she was sixteen. Her first job was at a small mom and pop diner a few blocks from her parent's house in Spitshire Grove. The diner was a landmark for the town, having passed from owner to owner since the 1920's. She began her career, as many teenagers do, as a hostess. Her duties included greeting customers as they came in the door, seating them at their tables, providing them with menus and water, busing after the meals were finished, and operating the cash register.

     When one of the cooks left to begin school at Princemoore University in nearby White River City, Brandie jumped at the opportunity to get her hands dirty in the kitchen. She had always enjoyed cooking at home and relished the chance at putting those skills to the test. During the holidays she had helped her grandmother prepare Thanksgiving and Christmas dinner, starting off as her assistant, but over time being given more and more responsibilities. Neither of her parents were much for cooking, preferring to either heat up TV dinners or go out to eat in the city. So the time she spent with her grandmother gave the two a special bond that still held to this day.

After graduating high school, Brandie decided to leave the diner behind and get a job in White River City. She knew there was a chance to increase her income by working at one of the big national chain stores, where the traffic and prices were higher than her small town of just under 1000 people. White River City, on the other hand, boasted a population of nearly 80,000 and even more when the university was in session. Not only that, there was far more to do when it came to entertainment, so Brandie decided to rent a small apartment after only a few months of working there.

While she wasn't old enough to get involved in the bar scene, she did manage to have plenty of fun going to parties with her co-workers. Many of them were students at PU, as the industry provided a flexibility of schedule that allowed for time to focus on studies. After the last of the customers had left and the restaurant was cleaned the servers and kitchen staff would meet up at one of the many parties going on in an off-campus neighborhood known as Drunken Acres. They would drink and smoke until the wee hours of the night, go home, pass out, then wake up and do it all over again. It had been a liberating experience for Brandie as she was exposed to people and cultures far different than the rural folks of Spitshire Grove.

It was at one of those raging Drunken Acre parties where she met Lee Upcraft. She had just turned 20, and he was celebrating his 21st

## The Virtue of Vices – Jeremy McShurley

birthday. Their courtship was a fast one, and after only three months of dating, the two were wed at the courthouse a week before Lee's deployment to Afghanistan. A couple of weeks later Brandie discovered she was pregnant. Her phone call to Lee about the child growing in her womb was the most joyous moment of their lives, and he spent the entire day running from soldier to soldier to spread the good news. But only two months later the couple's lives were shattered as she called again, this time to inform him about the miscarriage.

The impact took a huge psychological toll on Brandie. She entered into a deep state of depression and ended up missing work more often than not. Her employer eventually had to let her go, and she moved back home with her parents. After some time with her family and the emotional support they gave her she was finally able to recover from the loss. She and Lee purchased a trailer not too far from her parents, and things began to look positive once again. Her old boss even let her return to work, although the position was only part-time. Then, one night after coming home from work, Brandie found Lee waiting for her in their trailer, and learned he had been discharged from the army.

Brandie couldn't believe the news. As Lee explained it, the discharge fell somewhere between honorable and dishonorable. He was lucky to have avoided a court martial. That was all he could tell her. He would always say, "It's all political. I can't say anything else." But because of the type of discharge, Lee was unable to receive any sort of benefits from his service. There were nights where she would wake up to find herself alone in bed. Lee could almost always be found sitting on the couch, eyes wide open, muttering silently to himself.

He found work from time to time, mostly doing odd jobs around Spitshire Grove. On occasion he would pick up part-time or seasonal work, only to be fired or quit after a couple of months. Lee's transition back into civilian life was harder than he imagined. He came from a long line of servicemen, and he had planned on becoming a career soldier. His father practically disowned him after hearing about the discharge, and this did little to improve his self-esteem. Brandie thought things might start to turn around when she found out she was pregnant again. For a while, Lee found a purpose in his life, only to have it taken away when Brandie miscarried for the second time.

Her first miscarriage had been covered by Lee's benefits, but they were both uninsured for the second. This one was much worse than the first and Brandie had to spend several days at Princemoore Memorial Hospital as she recovered. As the medical bills piled up and the payment on the trailer and utilities started to run behind, they had to sell both their vehicles and buy an old clunker from one of Lee's buddies. So when Brandie received a call about a job opening at Pattywack's a few weeks ago, she jumped at the opportunity for the additional income.

The employees at her new job were either college students or a few long-timers. Some were restaurant vagabonds, spending their entire lives going from job to job without finding any sort of satisfaction. Besides the university and hospital there wasn't a lot of industry in White River City. A good portion of the former factory workers had to take whatever work they could. They ended up trading in twenty dollars an hour industrial manufacturing for minimum wage burger slinging. The decrease in

## The Virtue of Vices – Jeremy McShurley

disposable income cascaded throughout the city and began a cycle of lost jobs and closing businesses.

As the Pattywack's crew was leaving this evening, one of the line cooks stopped Brandie on the way to her car. He invited her to meet up with everyone at their regular hangout; a pool hall called Shooters. For years the staff had been going to the run down establishment on the southwest side of the city, even as new faces came and went. The patronage of Pattywack's cooks and servers had probably kept the place open over the last ten years, so the owners always made sure to save them a couple of tables on Friday nights. And the $3 pitchers of domestics and $2 well drinks didn't hurt the crew's wallets like the prices at the University Mall.

While Brandie herself only purchased a couple of drinks, her co-workers were generous with the rounds. Everyone played pool up until last call at 3 a.m., and then ended up hanging out in the parking lot for a while, passing around a flask and talking trash about customers and the management staff. Brandie even took a couple of hits off a joint, something she almost never did. The effects amplified the liquor, and she had to sit in her car for nearly half an hour before feeling sober enough to start her trek back to Spitshire Grove.

On a usual night going home, Brandie would have headed west on Oak Avenue out of White River City, crossed Highway 17, then turned south onto County Road 485. From there it was a left on Rigglesbey Street and then a right into Willow Crossing Mobile Home Park. But Brandie's fear of failing a breathalyzer had sent her home on an unusual route. Instead, she took the dark and curvy back roads, hoping to avoid as much traffic as possible. As she passed the sign for Spitshire Grove town limits, she relaxed a little bit, knowing she was less than ten minutes from her trailer.

Brandie noticed a set of headlights quickly approaching and slowed back down just under the speed limit. The vehicle came within a few feet of the back of Brandie's car, and she gulped when she thought the silhouette of police lights could be made out on the roof of the car. Her fears were confirmed when the night became illuminated by the flashing red and blue lights of a cop car.

She turned on her right blinker, slowly pulled over to the side of the road and put the car into park. "I swear to God I will never do this again if you get me out of this," she quietly prayed. Brandie then reached over to grab the registration from the glove box. She next retrieved her driver's license from her backpack and popped several breath mints in her mouth. After a minute or so the officer cautiously got out of the vehicle and began approaching the driver's side door with a hand on their weapon. At the last minute, Brandie sprayed some air freshener and used the hand crank to roll the window down.

The officer was a female with short, dark curly hair and a stocky build. "You have a tail light out," she explained. "I need your registration and ID." After giving her order, she shined a flashlight into the backseat.

Brandie did as commanded and sat upright and rigid with both hands visibly holding the steering wheel.

"This says the car is registered to a Craig Van Horne," the officer informed her.

"Yes," Brandie began. "We just bought it a little while back. We've been pretty broke lately and haven't been able to get it in our name. But I just got a second job, and I will take care of it on Monday," she explained.

"Wait. Brandie?" asked the officer.

Brandie turned towards the officer. She had been trying to keep her head turned slightly to the right to avoid breathing towards her. "Rose? Oh, I couldn't see you." Brandie started to think she might avoid a DUI. Officer Rose Hernandez had been going to Brandie's old diner since before she started working there. The owners gave cops and firemen a fifteen percent discount, which of course kept would-be robbers away and insured the fire engines would show up in record time.

"What happened to your car?" Rose asked. She had let her guard down and was now learning on the roof with one arm.

"We had to get rid of it. But like I said, I just got hired at Pattywack's so hopefully we can get rid of this piece of junk. You should come in sometime. I'll hook you up," Brandie offered.

"Have you been drinking?" asked Rose as she caught a whiff of booze in the air.

"I had a couple after work. But that was hours ago," Brandie lied. "First time out with the crew, ya know?"

"I still have to do my job, Brandie. But like Dad always says, 'If you don't blow, then you're free to go,'" she quoted her father, the chief of police in Spitshire Grove. She started to head back to the cruiser to get the breathalyzer.

Brandie began whispering a string of curses that would have made a sailor blush. If she blew over the limit, she would be spending the rest of the night in jail. Lee didn't have the money to bail her out and most likely she would lose her job and possibly her liquor license. She started thinking about every trick she had read online about beating a breathalyzer. In the background, she heard the sounds of Rose's radio streaming through the air.

Rose quickly returned to Brandie's car empty handed. "You are one lucky son of a bitch. They think they spotted the Beanstalk shooter headed south on 17." Rose wagged her finger at Brandie. "Don't ever, ever, do this again."

Brandie was on the verge of tears. "Oh my God. I swear, Rose. I swear, never again. I owe you," she promised.

Officer Hernandez ran back to her vehicle and shouted, "Don't think I won't cash in on that one day!" The cruiser made a quick three point turn and sped off, lights slowly disappearing into the distance.

Brandie drove the short distance home in a cold sweat. She noticed the blue flickering light of the television coming through the front window as she pulled into the drive. After grabbing her backpack she walked towards the door, hoping that Lee still had some cigarettes. Not generally a smoker, Brandie was certainly going to have one after her run in with the law.

She stepped into the house and noticed the living room was empty. The TV was playing sports highlights. Brandie spotted several beer cans sitting on the coffee table. She cursed under her breath, as Lee had promised he wouldn't drink until he found another job. Brandie grabbed the remote from the armrest of the couch and started flipping through the local news channels, looking for updates on the Beanstalk Café shooting.

Next to a shot glass was a crumpled pack of smokes. Brandie pulled one out and scrounged around for a lighter, stopping when she heard the sound of the toilet flush. She muted the television, picked up one of the empty beer cans and stood waited for her husband to come into the room.

Lee walked out of the narrow hallway and upon seeing his wife, stumbled over to give her a hug. She stepped to the side. "So, I assume you found work," she asked, holding the beer can towards Lee.

"Nope. But it's ok..." he gleefully explained, slurring slightly.

"You are drunk as a skunk," she angrily tossed the beer can onto the table, knocking down the small pile. The move revealed a lighter that she quickly picked up and used to light the cigarette. "I can't believe this. I just got done working a double, and you're here getting wasted alone. You promised." She stared directly into Lee's eyes. "You pinky swore."

"Don't be mad. Come here," Lee requested with a gesture as he walked into the kitchen. There were several envelopes laid out on the small, round kitchen table next to the wall. "Here," he continued to call for her.

Brandie reluctantly followed her husband into the other room as she deeply inhaled nicotine and tried not to scream.

Lee opened the refrigerator and presented its contents as though he was a model on a game show. "Ta da." The fridge was completely filled. The last time that much food was inside was when Lee's paychecks from the Army were still coming in. "I got milk, juice, veggies, lunch meat, some chicken. And a couple of steaks."

He grabbed Brandie by the wrist and pulled her towards the pantry that was also full. Lee continued listing off inventory, "Chips, beans, corn, a bunch of soups. Oh, and your favorite, butterscotch chip cookies."

Brandie stood silently, her mouth open in shock. "How? What?"

"That's not all." Lee walked to the kitchen table and started picking up different envelopes, showing Brandie the cash in each one. "Electric, water, cable, house payment. And next month's hospital bill."

"Did you rob a bank? Win the lottery?" Brandie asked still in shock.

"Yes. The lottery part. I borrowed Andy's truck to go drop off applications in town. Coming back I stopped to grab a pop. They had some deal where you got a free 22oz if you bought a scratch off, so I figured, what the hell? I won fifty bucks!"

"This is way more than fifty dollars, Lee," Brandie noted as she started counting the money in the envelopes.

"And then I went to Dr. Graham's poker game cleaned everybody out," he admitted with the speed of an auctioneer.

Brandie tossed an envelope back onto the table then grabbed her husband around the waist. She started crying as she dropped down to her knees, bringing Lee with her. He wrapped his arms around her shoulders and pulled her in, kissing her sweetly on the top of the head. After a few minutes of catharsis, Brandie pulled away from their embrace.

"Lee Franklin Upcraft. I love you. I love you so much," she confessed, then rested her head on his chest.

"I love you too, baby. More than anything in the whole world." Lee gently rocked his wife as they sat together in the middle of the kitchen floor.

Brandie eventually stood up and walked into the living room. On the floor next to the couch was a bottle of rum with a little bit left in the bottom. She came back, opened the cabinet and pulled out two plastic cups. Brandie poured a small amount into each cup then handed one to Lee. "Looks like we both got lucky today," she said then downed the rum in one gulp.

Lee quickly followed suit.

Brandie returned to the living room, sat down on the couch and started flipping through the channels until she found a movie she wanted to watch. Lee shortly joined her and put his arm around her shoulder.

"You probably want to get to bed, yeah?" he asked.

"No. Not yet. But we're gonna hit the sack early tomorrow," Brandie informed him with raised eyebrows.

"Yeah? Why's that?" he asked, knowing that Brandie was a perpetual night owl.

Brandie leaned her head onto the back of the couch and looked up towards the ceiling. "Because we are getting up Sunday morning and dragging our sorry asses to church."

**Extremism** - *(ik-stree-miz-uhm)*
Fanatic interpretation of a point of view that is out of the mainstream

As the red on-air light went black, Leon Joneway removed his headphones while his producer, Gordy, began playing a set of commercials for the current break. Leon stood up from his chair and stretched out his back and neck. It was going to be a long day and Leon had no intention of cramping up this early into the show. *The Leon Joneway Show* was a popular news and talk program broadcast out of Spitshire Grove Studios just southwest of White River City. The show usually ran from six in the morning until one in the afternoon, but today they were broadcasting a twenty-four hour marathon. Leon had wanted to do this for years, and the opportunity presented itself a few weeks ago when a couple of less popular shows were canceled.

Leon looked into the window of the production booth, noticed that Gordy was gone, and assumed he was taking a bathroom break. They were at the top of the fourth hour of the marathon and he knew there was going to be several minutes of commercials. Leon grabbed his notes for the upcoming hour, and starting reading through them as he paced around the studio. The studio was smaller than his previous one in White River City but the overhead was a lot lower and the owners of the station had given him considerably more control of the creative content since he had come here three years ago. Plus, the residents of Spitshire Grove were a little more conservative than a lot of the folks in White River City and he felt more at home surrounded by like-minded individuals.

## The Virtue of Vices – Jeremy McShurley

He had been born and raised in White River City, growing up during 70's and eventually becoming a local football star at Eastside High. He was hotly recruited after graduating in 1987 and the city was sorely disappointed when he decided to play at rival Harrold State rather than for the hometown Princemoore Pumas. Leon was a rarity among athletes, as he received both an academic and a football scholarship, choosing to major in political science and minor in journalism. After graduating from college he was signed as a free agent with the Lake Land Harbor Stallions where he played five years as a backup defensive back before retiring. Unlike most former professionals, who spent through their wealth in a matter of years, Leon had lived frugally, saving and investing as to avoid struggling his whole life as his parents had done.

Although he was offered several positions as a sports analyst, he turned all of them down. While he understood the importance football had in shaping his life and providing for him financially, he was more interested in pushing the ideology of his childhood hero, Ronald Reagan. His parents were lifelong Democrats, and his father was a union man through to the bone. But when his father's factory closed down and his pension mysteriously "dried up", Leon began to seek alternatives to the liberal agenda.

Pouring through the conservative literature of authors like Goldwater, Rand, Buckley, and Buchanan, Leon concluded that small government, trickle-down economics, and a strong military were the best solutions to America's problems. In his younger years he was more liberal on the social issues, but after getting married, starting a family, and returning to the church, his social views started falling in line with his conservative fiscal and security convictions. By the time he retired from football, he had formed a political philosophy that remained with him to this day.

His radio career began at a small station in Lake Land Harbor on a show called *In Your Heart*, a play off of a Barry Goldwater campaign slogan. The show was broadcast in the middle of the night but its recordings were downloaded over the Internet by fans from all over the nation. Leon's constant attacks on President Clinton garnered tremendous admiration from the conservative movement and he was poised to become the next Rush Limbaugh. But the War on Terror changed the political environment entirely as much of the country became unified behind President Bush. And without a liberal government in Washington to bash, Leon started striking out at any targets he could find. His ratings started falling and he spent the next several years bouncing around from station to station. When his mother became ill, he secured a job in White River City to be closer to her. Then, the political pendulum swung again, President Obama was elected, and Leon's career found new fodder.

It didn't take long after Obama's election for Leon to realize the rising influence of the Tea Party Movement. He actively promoted their stances and provided their members with an outlet on his show. His ratings slowly began to climb again, much to the chagrin of the progressives at nearby Princemoore University. It was around this time when he began having more left-leaning guests on the show, not so much to provide a balanced perspective, but instead to create a volatile environment where tempers were certain to flare. His technique worked, and *The Leon*

*Joneway Show* became syndicated in 2011, the same year he moved into the Spitshire Grove studio.

A production assistant named Molly poked her head into the room. "Mr. Joneway, is it time to send the next segment's guests in?"

Leon looked up from his notes then into the production booth. He noticed Gordy was just sitting back down. "That would be fine, Molly. Thank you." He took his seat, adjusted his microphone, and put his headphones back on.

Gordy came over the headset, "We're back in 5, 4, 3…"

"Welcome back to the 24-hour marathon of *The Leon Joneway Show;* this is your host, Leon Joneway. We have some wonderful guests in the studio this hour as we'll be discussing a topic that's very important to many of our listeners and to a lot of Americans in general."

Molly was helping Leon's guests into their seats and getting them set up with their headsets and microphones as Leon welcomed his listeners. The two guests sat next to one another across the table from their host. Each one of them had their own set of papers and note cards and they began to arrange them on the table as Leon continued.

"I'd like to begin by reading from a couple of different passages from two completely opposite worldviews. Here's the first one. '. And God made the beast of the earth after his kind, and cattle after their kind, and every thing that creepeth upon the earth after his kind: and God saw that it was good. And God said, Let us make man in our image, after our likeness: and let them have dominion over the fish of the sea, and over the fowl of the air, and over the cattle, and over all the earth, and over every creeping thing that creepeth upon the earth. So God created man in his own image, in the image of God created he him; male and female created he them. And God blessed them, and God said unto them, Be fruitful, and multiply, and replenish the earth, and subdue it: and have dominion over the fish of the sea, and over the fowl of the air, and over every living thing that moveth upon the earth.'"

After a brief pause he continue, "And here's our second passage. 'We have reason to believe, as stated in the first chapter, that a change in the conditions of life, by specially acting on the reproductive system, causes or increases variability; and in the foregoing case the conditions of life are supposed to have undergone a change, and this would manifestly be favourable to natural selection, by giving a better chance of profitable variations occurring; and unless profitable variations do occur, natural selection can do nothing. Not that, as I believe, any extreme amount of variability is necessary; as man can certainly produce great results by adding up in any given direction mere individual differences, so could Nature, but far more easily, from having incomparably longer time at her disposal'."

Leon looked up from his notes to make sure his guests were fully situated. "Two quite different views on one of our most common universal questions; 'Where did we come from'? Anthony Ramirez is a biology professor at Princemoore University. Thank you for joining us this morning."

"It's my pleasure, thank you for having me, Leon. And I'd like to say hello to any of my students who are listening. Remember, extra credit for those of you who turn in a five-page essay on today's debate by next Wednesday."

## The Virtue of Vices – Jeremy McShurley

"We also have state senator Walter Michelson. Senator Michelson has recently introduced legislation that would allow for parents to decide whether their children should take biology or Creationism classes," Leon began.

Senator Michelson interrupted, "Actually, I need to correct you real quickly, Leon. Creationism implies imposing religion into the classroom, which is currently unconstitutional. We would like parents to be given a choice between evolution and Intelligent Design."

Professor Ramirez chimed in, "Senator, please. Everyone knows that Intelligent Design is just a new coat of paint on an old, worn out fence. There is absolutely no evidence whatsoever that life on Earth was 'designed' by anything."

The senator shuffled through his notes and responded, "Here's some 'evidence' for you, professor. According to recent polling, 42% believe God created humans as they are, while 31% say God has a hand in evolution. Only 19% believe that God has no part in the evolution process. By my numbers, that's 73% in favor of God and 19% in favor of atheism."

The professor shook his head in frustration, "That's not at all what those numbers are saying. Atheism and science are not the same thing. I have plenty of colleagues who go to church on Sunday and spend Monday through Friday in the lab. I have no problem studying scripture in church. But we need to be preparing our children for a future in science and technology and Intelligent Design or Creationism, or whatever else you want to call it won't provide that. The Catholic Church has accepted evolution. Why won't Evangelicals do the same?"

Leon jumped into the fray, "I'd like to mention one thing here. The first passage I read is beautifully written, like poetry. But the second sounds very cold and calculated, almost soulless."

"That's right," said Professor Ramirez, "It does sound like poetry. Because it is poetry. The Bible is a very well written book, with lots of stories, moral lessons, and some history. But that doesn't equate it with forming a hypothesis, testing that hypothesis, then either supporting or refuting the evidence. You know? The scientific method."

"If there weren't some designer of life on Earth, then how do you explain the complexities of the genetic code, professor? You can't really believe that a bunch of goo decided to form together and start making babies, do you? How do you explain lungs and the heart? Fingers and toes? And especially, how do you explain the brain?" The senator sat back and waited for a response.

"I will do my best in giving the short version, seeing as we only have about an hour. Is that right, Leon?"

"I certainly wish we had more time. I'm really enjoying this conversation and I hope our listeners are as well. We'll open up the phone lines here in a bit. But go ahead professor," Leon prompted.

"Senator, this 'goo' you refer to is best known as primordial soup. The early Earth was a hostile environment, far different from the present. The composition of the atmosphere and electrical activity allowed chemicals to form monomers. Over time those monomers became more complex polymers to form the foundation of our DNA."

"That sounds a little like magic to me," the senator retorted.

"No, not magic, science. Although it was Arthur C. Clarke who said 'Any sufficiently advanced technology is indistinguishable from magic.' Thousands of years ago we didn't understand biology the way we do today. People wanted answers so their sages and shamans created stories to set their minds at ease. The Bible gives us an insight into man's thinking at the time. From an anthropological and historical perspective I find it fascinating to see how our ancestors dealt with the mysteries of life. We're talking about a process that is billions of years in the making." Professor Ramirez took a breath, believing to have made a significant point.

"The jury is still out on that. We don't really know how old the Earth is. Some say it's only a few thousand years old."

"Yes. You. You say that and anyone who decided to take someone's mathematical calculations from a single source instead of measuring radioactive decay. The evidence shows that the further you dig into the Earth's crust the more simple life forms we find. The fossil record isn't perfect, but it's the best thing we have. What Darwin was saying is that certain species are going to exhibit new traits from time to time. If the environment is conducive to those traits, those animals will pass on those genes to future generations. If not, then that line will die off."

"If that's true, then why are there still monkeys? If we descended from monkeys then there shouldn't be any monkeys around today, according to your theory," Senator Michelson asked, believing to have backed the professor into a corner.

Professor Ramirez laughed. "This is one of the most common misconceptions about evolution.

We didn't 'descend' from monkeys. Millions and millions of years ago a common ancestor of monkeys and apes split off from one another. That same thing happened with apes and humans between 4-12 millions of years ago."

Leon broke into the conversation. "This is just fascinating. And I believe our listeners have found it just as fascinating. We have Justin from White River City with a question."

*"Do you believe in Hell, professor?"*

"I. I'm not really sure. As a cultural concept, certainly. Religion has used the idea of a place of torment for centuries. It was a control mechanism for a time when we were less developed both morally and technologically. But I've seen no evidence of either life after death or any sort of realm beyond the physical."

*"And what about you, Senator Michelson? Do you believe in Hell?"*

"Oh, of course. I believe that we are born into sin and through the redemption of our Lord and Savior, Jesus Christ, that those sins can be absolved. By accepting Jesus into my life, I have avoided eternal damnation."

"That's an interesting question, Justin," Leon interrupted. "But we're talking about Creationism versus evolution. Do you have a question on those topics?"

*"The Bible is the written word of God brought to us through his only Son, Lord Jesus. It is the divine word, uncorrupted by Satan and his evil minions. Satan is known to whisper temptation into our ears on a daily basis. He had his minions bury bones in the ground to deceive us and lead us away from God's light. How is it you accept the word of a man, Charles Darwin, over the word of God?"*

## The Virtue of Vices – Jeremy McShurley

Professor Ramirez looked over at both Leon and Senator Michelson. Even the senator's eyes had widened a bit at the question, as his rhetoric was more for political gain than of personal conviction.

"Well, Justin, was it? This is a free country, and you are more than welcome to believe that, what did you say? Satan's minions put bones in the ground. Personally, I choose to believe in the scientific evidence in front of me. But new evidence is always being discovered, and that changes the narrative. To me, that's what makes science so exciting. But as far as I know, Satan has never whispered in my ear and I find Charles Darwin's ideas to be an integral part of what I do."

"Hi there, Justin. I too struggle every day with temptation. The Devil's handiwork appears to us in many ways. That's why I look to the Good Book to help guide me. Man makes mistakes all the time. God is the one who's infallible," the senator concluded.

*"You should probably read up a little bit on Hell professor. Because that's where you'll be going someday."*

Leon turned around towards Gordy and made a slicing motion across his throat with the tips of his fingers then spun his chair back around towards the microphone. "Wow, thank you, Justin. As I said at the beginning of the segment, this is a topic of interest to many people who all have their own individual viewpoints. We're going to continue our discussion after we return from this short commercial break."

**Fixation** – (fifik-sey-shuhn)
Extreme level of focus or obsession on a person, object or idea

High heels in hand, Brittany's legs pumped in unceremonious fashion as she made her way down the broken sidewalk, dodging the jagged and uneven pavement that had been lifted into a jumble of unnatural obstacles by roots many decades old. Normally her athletic training would have allowed her to endure the strain, but the infusion of adrenaline and concern put her body into a state of uncomfortable distress. Her reactions were comprised of both fear and compassion. She was running from 103 Hort Street. Just a few moments ago her sorority sister had sent her a message.

**Amanda T.**: *Been txting and calling for an hour. @ corner of Wilber and Steight. It's an emergency!*

Brittany's sprint slowed down to a saunter as she approached the group of smokers outside of her destination.

"You guys seen Amanda?" she asked, slightly panting.

"Who?"

"Nevermind." Brittany moved away, opening the gate into the backyard. "Amanda!"

"There, you are!" Amanda walked away from a small campfire.

"Are you alright? What's going on?"

"I've been texting and calling you forever. We have that show to see."

"Show?"

"Yeah. You said a month ago you'd come with me to see Caleb Brown," Amanda reminded Brittany, gesturing frantically.

The Virtue of Vices – Jeremy McShurley

"Are you kidding me? You said this was an emergency!" Brittany was overwhelmed with outrage, her normally passive personality transforming into a slew of disbelief and abhorrence.

"It is an emergency," Amanda reminded her. "This is Caleb Brown. It's not like he comes back to town every week. Don't you remember?"

Brittany tried to think back to the conversation she and Amanda had at the beginning of the semester, but her memory was fuzzy. "I guess," she finally agreed.

From a distance, Justin watched the girl with short brown hair and Amanda as they walked away from the rocking party. Justin had made many a coffee for Amanda in his time slinging caffeinated drinks for the unforgiving patrons of The Beanstalk Cafe. He had enjoyed calling out her name to let her know the order was complete. Despite having worked there for many years, the owners finally let Justin go two days ago for his persistent preaching to both employees and customers. Only a few minutes before, Justin's latest attempt at proselytizing to the sinners of Princemoore University had ended in failure yet again.

"'Love is patient, love is kind. It does not envy, it does not boast, it is not proud. It is not rude, it is not self-seeking, it is not easily angered, it keeps no record of wrongs. Love does not delight in evil but rejoices with the truth. It always protects, always trusts, always hopes, always perseveres. Love never fails. And now these three remain: faith, hope and love. But the greatest of these is love.'"

Justin quickened his pace but tried to stay far enough behind the two girls as to not draw their attention. He could hear they were arguing about something.

"Well I'm sorry if I ruined your chances of getting laid tonight, Britt."

"It wasn't like that. We really hit it off. He's cute, super smart, and seems to have a plan for his life. How many guys our age know what they want to do? They can't even decide on pizza toppings half the time." Brittany's mind drifted back to her conversation with Nick. While she believed in love at first sight, she had never experienced it before. Yet, during their brief chance encounter, she noticed the constant fluttering of butterflies in her stomach, a feeling she thought had ended in middle school. She could have sworn there was electricity that connected their two hearts, gently pulling them towards one another like opposite poles of a magnet.

"Is there some reason we're not driving to Holidaze?" asked Brittany, her bare feet aching.

"If I have my car then how do I expect Caleb to give me a ride home? Or maybe he'll just let me sleep with him inside *Beowulf*," Amanda fantasized, her eyes drifting into the sky.

"*Beowulf?*" Brittany couldn't imagine what in the world Amanda was talking about.

"That's the name of his RV. Caleb needs his private space so he can meditate. That's why he makes the rest of the band ride in the tour bus." Amanda knew everything there was to know about Caleb Brown, having read all the articles she could get her hands on. The walls of her bedroom were covered with his posters and her music playlist contained every one of his songs. She followed him on all his social media and even spent last summer following him around on tour, although never getting a chance to meet him. Caleb was a local kid who made it big, and he rarely played smaller venues like Holidaze. But because of the intimacy of the music

## The Virtue of Vices – Jeremy McShurley

hall and smaller security detail, she thought this was her best chance to hook up.

"What time does the show start?" asked Brittany.

"Ten-thirty, but those things never start on time. There's a couple of other bands, but I don't know who they are and really don't care. I just need to see my Caleb." Again Amanda began to fantasize, thinking about leaving school to go on the road, getting married, and having all the little musician babies Caleb wanted.

Brittany sighed. She had heard Amanda play Caleb's music for countless hours over the years. Caleb's music was initially juvenile and angst-ridden like the songwriter himself. As they started touring with larger acts, the more mature musicians who surrounded them influenced the band. But the most significant change to their style came a few years ago after Caleb had a sojourn in the desert of the American Southwest. He returned with a new vision and writing style. When interviewed about his experience, Caleb told the reporter he "had been cleansed." While Brittany thought the band was talented, she didn't share Amanda's level of fascination and would rather be back talking with Nick. But she did promise to come, and Brittany was someone who kept to her word.

The two girls turned left onto the Jefferson Street Bridge that crossed the White River and led from the Princemoore University campus to Downtown. Jefferson Street came off of Princemoore Avenue, a beautiful tree-lined road that curved along the river and connected campus to the luxurious East Bank District. The west side of town was like another world, and the only thing that kept Downtown from decaying like the rest of this side of the river was the constant influx of students looking to party. There were attempts to renovate Downtown in the 1960s but with the university on the other side, decades of economic depression allowed for most of Downtown to fall into disrepair.

    White River City didn't have much of a skyline, but it was hard to miss the giant Princemoore Building that stood at the heart of the business district. Brittany stared up at the building's top, trying her best to ignore Amanda as she droned on and on about becoming the future, Mrs. Caleb Brown. They made their way over to Main Street and finally reached Holidaze, passing several busy bars on the way. There were certain parts of Downtown where the students were constantly warned to avoid, and the girls knew the safe routes very well.

    Brittany leaned up against one of the pillars at the entrance and put her shoes back on.

    "You coming?" Amanda pleaded, her excitement growing at an exponential level.

    "Yeah."

    The loud thumping beats of electronic dance music and the subtropical rainforest feel of the room gave Justin second thoughts about coming here. The music was so deafening that it was tough to hear himself think, but he had made up his mind that he was going to finally try to talk to Amanda. He remembered noticing her golden cross necklace a long time ago and had complimented her on it. Justin had tried several times to speak with her about Lord Jesus while she was at the cafe, but his work duties and her reluctance to respond kept that from happening. After a few apologies and excuse me's he was able to get close to the dance floor where most of the patrons had congregated. He scanned the crowd for a bit. Then, Justin finally saw Amanda. He slowly backed himself against the wall and watched as she danced and bounced to the pulsating rhythms of techno-tribal songs.

"You want another drink!?" Amanda yelled to Brittany.

"What!?"

Amanda leaned in. "Drink! Do you want one!?"

"Actually, I think that first one just went through me. I'm going to hit the ladies room!" she informed her friend into her ear.

There were a few girls in line ahead of her, so Brittany pulled out her phone. She began mindlessly looking at her newsfeed, making a few comments here and there as the line moved forward. After a couple of minutes she made her way into the bathroom and sat down on one of the toilets. Just as she was about to put her phone back in her purse it made a tone indicating an instant message.

**Nick Stone**: *Hi! I hope you don't mind me cyberstalking you. Where'd U go?*

**Brittany Stoffer**: *Not at all :) I forgot I was supposed to see some band w my friend. We're at Holidaze if you want to join us.*

**Nick Stone**: *I would like to see you again. But I can't stand that Caleb guy. He's such an assclown.*

**Brittany Stoffer**: *lol My friend's totally in love with him.*

**Nick Stone**: *Might make my way there l8r. U got plans after?*

**Brittany Stoffer**: *not really*

**Nick Stone**: *how bout we meet up at Beanstalk?*

**Brittany Stoffer**: *sounds good*

**Nick Stone**: *hit me up after the show if I don't c u there*
**Brittany Stoffer**: *k*

As Justin watched Amanda grind and gyrate up against several different guys, moving back and forth between each one without an ounce of dedication to any, he realized the cross she wore wasn't a symbol of devotion. Instead, it was just another piece of jewelry, an idol of adultery, and the mark of one of Satan's Deceivers. Each passing moment his teeth clenched a bit tighter as did his fists. He felt someone next to him touch his shoulder.

"You ok, man?" asked a guy wearing a Caleb Brown shirt while pointing at Justin's hand.

Something was dripping from his knuckles, and when he opened his hands, he noticed a smear of blood on each palm. "Stigmata. Stigmata!" He turned to the Caleb Brown fan. "Do you know what this means? It's time. I have received my sign from Lord Jesus!" Justin pushed his way through the crowd and out the doors of the music hall. He could be heard yelling "Stigmata!" as he ran down the street and disappeared around the corner.

"Stigmata?" One of the bouncers said. "Those guys played last week."

The intermission dance music was now off, and scores of people made their way towards the stage. Amanda pulled Brittany by the hand and squirmed through the masses to get to the front. The curtains opened and the music hall filled with the cheers and shouts of anticipating fans. Most of the stage was dark except for a pale white light that illuminated Caleb. He was wearing tight fitting jeans and a traditional Native American shirt while

# The Virtue of Vices – Jeremy McShurley

standing behind a keyboard. The slow sounds of synth-strings began playing through the speakers.

"He's starting with 'Quiver,'" noted Amanda, clapping and bouncing up and down.

Caleb began singing,

> I dream of you; Think of you; Everyday of my life
>
> You're my constant fascination; My destiny
>
> I yearn for you; Wait for you; Cuts just like a knife
>
> I never thought I'd feel so much intensity

The drummer clicked his sticks three times, indicating a tempo change and the rest of the band joined in with distorted electric guitar and low, rumbling bass.

> It's the way: You look at me out of the corner of your eye
>
> It's the way: I take a backseat to that other guy
>
> It's the way; It's the way; It's the way

As the song entered the chorus, the entire crowd began to sing along. Even Brittany mouthed the lyrics, having heard it a thousand times blaring out of Amanda's stereo.

> I start to quiver, shiver, all the times of the day
>
> It's like an earthquake, tsunami, I don't want to go away
>
> I start to quiver, shiver; and it's all because of you

Caleb grabbed a guitar from off of a stand and started into a blistering solo, raising the shouts of fans into screams of amazement. After finishing the solo with a long vibrato note, he flung the guitar behind his back. Caleb and the crowd then went into another chorus. The song ended as it had begun, with a single light, and slow synth-strings fading into silence. The crowd cheered and clapped, and Caleb went to put his guitar back on the stand.

During this time, Amanda reached under her shirt and unclasped her bra strap. Before the show, she had written her phone number into both cups, and once she had removed it, flung the undergarment onto the stage. Caleb clasped his hands together and bowed, then pick up the bra and hung it over his microphone stand.

"This next one is called 'Hurting Season,'" Caleb announced, and once again the band started playing another crowd favorite.

Throughout the show, Brittany made several trips to the bar, leaving Amanda to fawn over her future imaginary husband. By the fifth visit she was starting to feel a little inebriated, so she switched to drinking water instead. Plus, Brittany didn't want to be too drunk when she met back up with Nick after the show. She brought Amanda a whiskey sour, and then began searching around Holidaze to see if Nick had managed to show up yet. She then checked her phone for messages and after not finding any, walked outside to cool off.

Other than a few smokers, the patio was pretty devoid of people. Most were inside, either dancing to the jams or grabbing a drink. Brittany picked a seat at one of the empty tables and again pulled her phone out of her purse. After making a status update she set the phone down, glancing at it periodically. She sipped on her water, trying to rehydrate as best she could. Brittany wasn't much of a drinker, as it tended to have a negative effect on her training during practice. She was hoping to make captain next year, as she would be one of only three seniors on the volleyball team. Princemoore

## The Virtue of Vices – Jeremy McShurley

University had put together a great program over the last few years, and it was the main reason she chose to come here.

While she had always excelled at athletics, her intellectual curiosity was self-admittedly low on her list of priorities. She was a good student, needing to keep her grades up to maintain her athletic scholarship, but until she met Nick earlier in the evening, she didn't get a lot of academic stimulation. Most of her friends were the same way. As an athlete, her time was dedicated to working out and watching game tapes. Her parents had been athletes as well, and she just assumed she would enter the family business. Brittany's dad played minor league baseball for a number of years, and her mom had been a track star in high school and college. But as she recollected the conspiracy theory laden conversation she had with Nick at the Hort Street house, she began to question her future.

Brittany had changed her major already several times and was currently finishing up her core classes. If she didn't figure out something soon, she would have to settle for a basic, run of the mill, liberal arts degrees. Although there weren't many opportunities to make money as a professional player, she did often consider trying the beach volleyball circuit. Not only would it give her a chance to do something she loved and was already good at, but she would also be able to travel the world. Having grown up in a house of athletes and being in sports clubs since she was a kid, there were a lot of experiences she felt she had missed out on. While her friends spent their summers going to camp and swimming at the gravel pit, she was in the gym working on her skill set for next season. The efforts were worth it, as it was paying for her schooling, but yet again she found herself thinking of Nick and his plans for "world domination."

The screen on Brittany's phone lit up and it vibrated against the plastic tabletop. She reached for the phone so quickly she almost knocked it off.

**Amanda T.**: *where are you? momma needs her drinky*

Brittany's shoulders lowered in disappointment, and her head dropped. She then shook her head and laughed, "What is wrong with you?" she whispered to herself. "You've known this guy, like, ten minutes and you're freaking out."

**Brittany Stoffer**: *outside getting some air. back in a sec*

It was getting close to midnight, and Brittany was wondering how much longer the show would last. She turned to one of the bouncers, "Are there any other bands playing tonight?"

"No, just dance music after," the bouncer informed her.

"How long does the main act usually play?"

"Depends."

"Great." Brittany put her phone into her purse again and downed the rest of her water. She slid her chair back under the table and turned to fetch Amanda another beverage.

"Hey there," said a familiar voice. Once again tiny butterflies began fluttering around in Brittany Stoffer's stomach as she felt her body quiver.

The Virtue of Vices – Jeremy McShurley

### **Gambling** - *(gam-bling)*
Taking actions of chance with the hope of a desirable outcome

"Mom. Mom!" The shouts of Melissa Graham's twelve-year-old son filtered down the stairs and into the kitchen.

"Stop yelling from the other room," Melissa commanded.

"You're yelling from the other room," her child retorted in a sarcastic tone.

Mrs. Graham set down the bowl of chip dip she had been mixing and marched to the foot of the staircase. At the top was her only child, a rambunctious young lad named Zander. Their eyes met, and she proceeded to give him The Stare. Young children often try to imitate The Stare, yet it is never mastered until they become parents themselves. There is no training manual for The Stare. It is a skill learned in the wilderness of human child rearing, most notably by the female of the species. On occasion, it can be substituted with or accompanied by its masculine counterpart, The Look.

"Can I have the wifi password?" Zander asked in a soft, passive tone.

"Have you finished your homework?" Melissa inquired.

There was a short pause. "Yes."

"Let me see it," Mellissa ordered. She extended her arm forward palm up. Her four fingers motioned like a fighter inviting their opponent into the ring.

"I might have a little more," Zander replied as his chin dropped towards his chest.

The Virtue of Vices – Jeremy McShurley

"The sooner you get it done, the sooner you can play your *Call Strike* or *Counter of Duty*, or whatever it's called," Zander's mom informed him.

Zander turned around and mumbled, "Ok. Fine."

Melissa returned to the kitchen. She was in the process of preparing snacks for her husband, Eric, and his poker-playing buddies. While the game's location had fluctuated over time, Friday night had been dedicated to poker for the last two decades. Melissa had seen different players come and go over the years. Hardly any of the original gang ever came, as they had started families of their own. On occasion, a regular would bring a new player along. The old regular would drop out, and the new player would take their place in the rotation.

Eric's grandfather had taught him to play when Eric would visit his grandparent's summer home in New Lake Falls up to the north. The only electricity for the cabin was a small generator, used for emergencies. Phone calls were made to and from the local police station, which also served as the post office. The two would play until the early morning, and then go fishing as the sun came up over the smooth blue-green lake behind the property.

Eric began his poker night tradition while still in high school and on through college. Not even med school could stop it, although playing time was limited to two hours. The game had only been canceled five times in over twenty years. The first was when Melissa, still his girlfriend at the time, got into a motorcycle accident. Eric stayed with her at the hospital the entire night. When she was still in traction the following week, Melissa insisted the game be played in her hospital room. The next cancellation was due to weather. The ice storm of the century, as it was touted on the news, whirled into White River City and shut down every business, school, and event for four days. Eric's friends insisted on coming, but he wouldn't risk them driving on the slick and dangerous roads.

The third time the game was canceled was for the birth of Zander. Last year Zander's birthday fell on a Friday and the family spent the entire afternoon at the zoo. Zander was so exhausted when he got home he couldn't stay awake even for cake. The guys came over a couple of hours later. Two years later was the next cancellation. According to Melissa, it shouldn't count, but because Eric couldn't remember the game he claimed it never happened. Melissa and Eric had begun his medical school graduation earlier in the day than everyone else. By the time the other players arrived, Eric was smashed. He somehow ended up winning that night; although there were rumors his buddies threw the game as a graduation gift.

The last time there wasn't a Friday night poker game was three years ago. Eric, Melissa, and Zander had flown down to Florida for Eric's grandpa's funeral. His death was a complete surprise, as Eric's grandfather was relatively healthy for a man in his 80s. He had slipped on the pier and hit his head on a nearby boat. The neighbors found him floating face down a few hours later.

"Say, 'bye bye, Papaw,'" Eric had instructed, holding little Zander while waving his tiny hand towards the casket.

Eric then gently set the first set of cards his grandpa had given him onto Papaw's still chest.

"What's that for, Daddy?" Zander asked.

"It's so Papaw can play cards with Jesus."

The front door to the Graham residence opened, and Dr. Graham walked in. He kicked his shoes off and slid them to the side. The doctor then walked into the kitchen to kiss his wife.

"How was golf?" she asked leaning backward to receive a peck on the cheek.

"Good. Won fourteen holes. I'll take that any day," Eric said as he peeled off his polo shirt and tossed it into the hamper in the nearby laundry room.

"Nice. Did you get the taco seasoning?" Melissa asked.

"Crap," her husband hissed. "No, I forgot all about it. Peter was being a real dickhead and I kind of got sidetracked," he explained.

"How much on the Dick-o-Meter?" she questioned, having known Peter Princemoore for several years.

"Seven, seven and a half," Eric responded with a twisting motion of his hand.

"Oh, so just above average?" Melissa chuckled.

"Yeah. But you should have seen that shot on thirteen," the doctor said with envy. He pulled out his phone and looked up a recipe online. After a couple of minutes, he started grabbing some seasonings from the cabinet. Eric then pulled a small plastic container out from under the counter and dumped the seasonings into it. He triumphantly handed the plastic container to his wife, "Taco seasoning."

Melissa smiled in satisfaction. "Someone's been watching *Chef Yolanda.*"

"It's *Chef YOLO.* As in 'You Only Live Once.' And yes I have," Dr. Graham proudly declared.

## The Virtue of Vices – Jeremy McShurley

Melissa stopped what she was doing and planted a loud, juicy kiss on her husband's lips. "Well, thank you, Chef Graham. If this doctor thing doesn't work out, you may have a backup career."

"We'll see." Eric began heading towards the door that led to the basement. Melissa caught him out of the corner of her eye,

"Don't forget to say hello to your child," she reminded him. "You know? The one who's going to put us in a nursing home if we don't love him enough."

Eric immediately switched directions and headed upstairs. He helped Zander out with a couple of math problems and then told him the wifi password because according to Zander, "Mom forgot it." Eric then finally made his way to the basement.

In the back corner was a small home recording studio with a mixing board, two electric guitars, a bass, an electric drum set, and three microphones. Eric had a colleague set it up for him a couple of years ago. He had picked up playing music in med school, hearing it would keep his fingers nimble and his mind sharp. He dabbled a bit, but mostly the studio gathered dust. Along the right wall was a small wet bar with a full size-fridge filled with craft and import beers. A 73-inch flat screen hung on the wall on the opposite side furnished with plenty of seating. Eric turned on the radio and began setting up the table for tonight's game.

*"...consensus."*

*"Yes, there is. Over 90% of scientists agree that climate change is caused by human activity. This is why I've started to bring a dictionary along with me when I get in these debates with climate change*

*deniers. 'Consensus. Agreement on an opinion shared by most or all of a group.'"*

*"That's still not 100%. Shouldn't we wait for all scientists to agree before we overreact?"*

*"We don't have time to wait. Ocean levels are rising. Billions of people live on the coasts. If we don't do something to stem the tide, we will witness a population displacement that we haven't seen since The Tower of Babel."*

*"Isn't all this talk really just a ploy by the United Nations to enact a carbon tax? Don't you think we're taxed enough already?"*

*"If we could get carbon emitters to reduce their output with or without a carbon tax I would be happy. I have no political agenda here. You, on the other hand, have accepted millions and millions of dollars from the oil, gas, and coal industries. Your agenda couldn't be more transparent."*

*"And without all these scare tactics about the end of the world, your funding would dry up. Wouldn't it, Mitch?"*

*"You're going about this all wrong. Scientists look at data and make predictions. Then, we seek grants to study that research. Politicians and lobbyists take money, and then tow the line for their contributors and employers. By the year 2100, the oceans are expected to rise 2-6 feet. What you call scare tactics, I call the largest challenge the human race has ever faced."*

*"And what if you're wrong? Scientists in the 1970s thought we were entering a new ice age."*

*"I will be elated to be wrong. If I'm wrong, Congressman, then I will buy you a steak dinner, and we can laugh about how ridiculous I sounded. But I don't believe I'm wrong, and I don't believe 90% of*

*the scientific community is wrong either. Quite honestly, that is not a risk I'm willing to take."*

*"Then how do you explain the exhaust from volcanoes…"*

"What's that, dear?" Eric asked as he turned down the volume.

"Did you give Zander the wifi password?" Melissa yelled down.

"He said you forgot it," Eric explained.

"No. I told him he could have it after he finished his school work," she replied.

Eric finished his set up and began his Slow Dad Walk. He went into his bedroom and then unplugged the wireless router. Ten seconds later he heard the shouts of disappointment coming from down the hall. Eric took his time as he headed towards Zander's room. Ignoring the "Keep Out" sign posted on Zander's door, he turned the handle and slowly opened it up. Zander turned around towards the door to come face-to-face with The Look.

Paul Kozlowski was in the process of tearing the flesh off the palm of his hand as he attempted to remove the top of a porter.

Dave Larson tossed him a bottle cap opener. "Here, Paul. That's not a twist-off, unlike that swill you normally drink."

"What's wrong with my Schmutziger? It's twice filtered." Paul responded, slightly offended.

Detective Tranche joined the hazing. "I heard that. Some guy named Klaus drinks a stout, then both kidneys filter it before he pisses it into your bottle." The room erupted in laughter.

"Can I grab one of these axes?" Dave called from across the room.

"Have at it," replied Eric.

Dave began noodling on one of the doctor's guitars. He spent a minute tuning, then started strumming some chords. Tranche turned on the television and began looking for a basketball game. Paul sat on a stool at the bar and called his daughter.

"Hi, honey. You girls ok? You ordered dinner yet? No? I'd say get the most for your buck. How many showed up? Then I'd vote pizza. I think Athena's has a family deal. There should be a coupon in the junk drawer. Then get Chinese. Well, then Cara's mom can host next time. Honey, it's not that hard. Do you want me to order for you? Ok. Ok. Tomorrow? Who's Kyle? Maybe. I think I should probably meet this guy first. We'll talk about it later. Ok. Ok. Love you too."

"That your daughter?" asked Dave. He leaned the guitar against the bar then sat down next to Paul.

"Yeah. Slumber party," Paul answered and rolled his eyes.

"How old is she now?" Dave inquired.

"Thirteen this year," Paul responded with a slight shudder.

"Oof. Better you than me." Dave poured two shots of whiskey and offered one to Paul.

"To teenagers." Both men knocked back their shots.

"Oh, come on!" shouted Tranche at the television. The detective was genuinely irate. He tossed the remote onto one of the chairs and stomped to the bar to grab an import.

"You got some money on that game, Tranche?" asked Paul.

"No. I'm just sick of these new rules. I remember when a guy would get elbowed in the face they'd just keep playing. Now they call all these sissy-ass fouls. Just let 'em play," Tranche ranted.

"Too much money," Dave noted. "I hate all these new rules to protect the quarterbacks. It's football not badminton. If you're getting paid twenty million dollars to throw a ball around for three hours a week, then take your shots and shut the fuck up."

"Oh, speaking of," Paul interjected as he pulled up his fantasy football league on his phone.

"No fucking way, Paul," Dave stated. "Last time you were on that thing all night. Give it here." Dave tried unsuccessfully to wrench Paul's phone from his hand.

Eric called out from the poker table. "You jackholes ready to lose some money?"

Paul, Dave, and Tranche joined the doctor who was in the process of shuffling cards.

"What's the game, Doc?" Tranche asked.

"Hold 'em?" Dr. Graham suggested. There was a general rebuke from the group. "Draw?" The players reluctantly agreed.

"Got room for one more?" asked a voice from the stairwell.

Everyone turned to see a young man wearing tan khakis and a blue button-up shirt. His hair was cut short, and he stood with a rigid posture.

"Sure," invited the doctor. "Glad you finally decided to join us, Lee. Have a seat."

Lee pulled up a chair, and the group moved over to give him room. He set down a large fountain drink on the table.

"You want a beer?" asked Paul.

"No thanks," Lee answered.

Eric began the introductions. "Lee, this is Paul. Dave. And you probably know Detective Tranche."

"Hi, nice to meet you," Lee said shaking everyone's hands. He looked at the detective. "You're not here to arrest us, are you?"

"Only if I lose," Tranche responded with a straight face.

"Lee does work on some of my rentals," the doctor informed the group. "I'll probably hit you up in a few weeks once the leaves start coming down."

"That'd be great," Lee responded. He turned back to the doctor. "I was hopin' the offer still stood. Won some money on a scratch off. Figured I'd stop by."

"We're here every Friday. You're welcome anytime, bud," Eric assured him.

The players cut to see who would deal first. It turned out to be Tranche.

"Five card draw. Nothing wild. Dollar ante," he announced.

The game started slowly as normal. Paul continued to check his fantasy league until Tranche grabbed the phone from him. Dave chatted about his upcoming gig in Las Vegas, which took up the conversation for a while. Lee remained quiet through the first few hands as he learned to read each player. Paul finally got his phone back when his daughter called to ask how much to tip the delivery driver. Eric began going over the history of each category of the beer in his refrigerator, while the group as a whole continued to razz Paul about his lack of palate.

"Well, shit boys," Dave announced. "I believe I'm whipped." He looked down at his chips and counted up seven dollars worth.

"C'mom," Paul said. "We're just getting started."

## The Virtue of Vices – Jeremy McShurley

Dave finished his last swig of beer and started gathering his things. "I think I'm gonna check on my boy, Dan. See what he's getting into. Doc, always a pleasure."

"You leave next week?" asked Eric.

"Week after," Dave answered. He dropped his remaining chips on Lee's pile. "Lee, nice meeting you. Good luck with the job search." Dave began singing a tune on the way up the stairs. The lyrics had something to do with having sex with Eric's wife.

"Feel like upping the ante? Five good?" prompted Tranche. No one disagreed. "Five it is."

The pace of the game picked up without Dave's constant banter. Paul plied Detective Tranche for advice about his daughter, Laurie. The detective's daughter, Amanda, was about ten years older than Laurie and Paul thought Tranche might know some pointers. Eric told Paul he should bring Laurie next time because Zander had recently begun showing an interest in girls. Paul said he would speak with Laurie's mother first.

Lee chimed into the conversation on occasion, mostly giving short responses to questions. He had slowly built up nearly three hundred dollars in chips and was on the verge of cashing in and putting that money towards bills. He took his two draw cards. His hand was a straight flush to the Jack. He could play it smart, pick up a few more dollars, and end the night on a high note. He and his wife Brandie could really use the money. Then again, everything sitting in front of him had come from spending a dollar on a lottery ticket a few hours ago. And Dr. Graham had said he'd have some work for him in a few weeks. Detective Tranche's face was stone cold. Paul fiddled with his chips. The doctor was watching the basketball game. Lee had made his mind up. He was all in.

The Virtue of Vices – Jeremy McShurley

**Hoarding** - *(hawr-ding)*
Compulsive acquisition and storage of objects that have little to no purpose or utility

Kim Feinhorn turned her flashers on as she rolled down the passenger window and coasted towards the sidewalk.

"Mr. Holland! Reginald!" She parked the car and jumped out, pursuing an older African-American gentleman wearing a brown suit and matching fedora.

"Damnit, woman! Now they got ya following me home?" he shouted with disdain as his pace increased.

"No. No, please wait," Kim pleaded as she sped up to walk beside him.

Mr. Holland began to speed up again, but a slight coughing fit slowed him down.

"I'm not here to try to understand what you're going through. I'd do things a little differently, but I respect your decision." Kim was happy to see Mr. Holland stop and turn to speak to her.

He took his hat off and wiped his sweaty brow. While he didn't want to admit it, the pace was too much, and this unexpected respite was very welcoming.

"Then just let me go home. I ain't got much time left, and I'd like that time to be on my own terms." Reginald Holland's bloodshot eyes filled with tears. As he tried to blink them away, a single stream flowed down his aged and wizened cheek, catching the bottom of his chin then silently falling to the sidewalk.

Kim choked back her own tears, pushing the lump in her throat down into the pit of her stomach.

"Let me give you a ride at least. I promise I won't say a word."

She kept her promise as she drove Mr. Holland towards his house on the north side of White River City. She fiddled with the radio for a moment, and then turned it off as Reginald continued to stare out the window. The two rode in silence, but it was a stillness that spoke louder than any inane conversation might have mustered. Kim knew this was probably the last time she would see him alive. She planned on going to his wake so she could meet the children and grandchildren he had briefly spoken about at the hospital. Kim would never have children, at least not the way nature intended. By a stroke of luck or curse, her ovaries never produced eggs, and it changed the way she looked at life forever.

Her one basic function as a life form was removed from existence. From that time onward, Kim Feinhorn gained an insight to other's pain that few people on this planet possess. Following her diagnosis, she combed through every medical book she could get. While she never found a cure for her dilemma, she did discover a love for health and science. Compared to her infertility, there were so many others who suffered a much darker fate. Instead of wallowing in sorrow, Kim dedicated herself to giving hope to others, as she understood that someone else's pain was never something that one could compare on any scale of human design.

"Up here on the right," Mr. Holland instructed.

Kim pulled into the driveway of a split-level house on Weaver Street. The neighborhood was old but well kept as the homes had passed from generation to generation. The tall maple trees out front gave a clue to the age of the property, but the exterior looked to be in perfect condition. Just a mile or so north was Santa Mesa, White River City's ever-expanding suburb, and this part of town benefited from being caught between where the wealthy worked and where they lived.

The garage door was open, and Kim noticed a young man who looked to be in his late teens to his early twenties. He had black hair that was pulled back into a ponytail and stood before the largest pile of cardboard boxes Kim had ever seen. The boxes stretched across the entire doorway and reached to the top. She started to question Mr. Holland if he knew the guy but Reginald was already getting out of the car. She turned the engine off and got out as well.

"Is there anything else I can do for you, Mr. Holland?"

He stopped making his way towards the front door and turned to face Kim. "Thank you for the ride, ma'am," was all he said as he disappeared into the front entrance of his house.

The young man laughed, "You don't know him very well, do you?"

"Not really. Just the last couple of days, and he was sedated for most of it. How do you know him?"

"Sedated? What happened?" The guy started moving the stack of boxes second from the left, setting them on the ground one by one.

"Neighbors noticed him collapsed by the mailbox and called 911. He…" Kim began to describe the details of his medical problems but instead kept the information private.

"I'm Nick, by the way," he extended his hand which Kim accepted.

"Kim."

"Nice to meet you," said Nick as he finished taking down the stack.

"So, how do you know Mr. Holland?"

"Oh, me and 'ole Reggie go way back."

Nick Stone was nothing at all like the rest of his family. His great-great-great grandfather, Jefferson Stone, had been one of White River City's first mayors. His great-uncle had served on the city council for years before being elected to Congress in the early 90s. After losing re-election to a Tea Party candidate, Douglas Stone retired. Even Nick's father, Max, was involved in politics, having been the county chairman for Hillary Clinton during the 2008 election. But Nick wanted nothing to do with any of it, pledging to use his knowledge of governance to bring the whole system crashing down.

His father had been a bit of a political late bloomer but became involved in local affairs after losing interest in sports during college. Max married his high school sweetheart following graduation and Nick was born four months later. Nick had been dragged from one political rally to the next growing up, and he was witness to the verbal chicanery and insincerity of the entire process. As a child during the Clinton years, Nick's family praised the wonderful policies put forth by the President and admired his ability to work with the Republican Congress. Of course, the Bush Administration brought nothing but sour remarks into the Stone household, and by the 2008 campaign, Nick was completely fed up with hearing about it.

A few weeks before the election, Nick and several buddies drove around town, stealing as many campaign signs as possible. They had managed to fill the bed of Nick's truck with several hundred before they were finally pulled over. It was played off as a

The Virtue of Vices – Jeremy McShurley

juvenile prank, and Nick and his friends were forced to put every sign back. Forty hours of community service was part of his punishment, a lot for a sixteen-year-old kid. Nick was assigned to a program called Generations, a service where teenagers were paired with a senior citizen to help them with their daily tasks.

"Come on in, if you dare," Nick stepped into the darkened garage. He clapped twice and the garage lit up, although calling it a garage was a stretch. It looked more like a labyrinth, as though fifteen second-hand stores had been squished into a jar.

"Oh, my God," was all Kim could manage to utter.

"You should have seen it before I got here." Nick proceeded to tell Kim the story of how he had been assigned to Reggie when he was a teenager. Even after completing his program, he continued to return several times a week after school and on the weekends. Although the two were 50 years apart in age, they found common ground in their disdain for a corrupt and inequitable system.

"What does he do with all this stuff?" asked Kim as she explored the garage. Plastic shelves were evenly spaced throughout, giving just enough room to squeeze beside each one. They had been organized by category and labeled appropriately. The inventory comprised of canned and boxed food, magazines, newspapers, holiday decorations, office supplies, lamps, toiletries, stereos, drinking glasses, and an assortment of smaller electronic devices.

"Nothing. He barely comes out here," Nick explained as he walked around carrying a clipboard.

"This is insane. There's probably thousands of dollars worth of crap lying around," Kim estimated.

"Oh, there's more inside," Nick said with raised eyebrows. "When I came here about six years ago everything was in random piles. I asked Reggie what he wanted me to do and he said, 'Go to Hell.' I figured the garage looked like hell so I just started cleaning."

"He didn't want you here?" Kim asked as she flipped through a magazine from 1959.

"His daughter signed him up for the Generations program. He didn't even know about it 'til I showed up one day." Nick hung the clipboard on a nail beside the doorway into the house.

The door opened ajar, and Reggie stuck his head out. "You plannin' on makin' me soup anytime soon?" he asked looking at Nick.

"Be right in, Reg," Nick answered.

Mr. Holland noticed Kim standing nearby. "You still here? Ain't ya got nothin' better ta do?" Before Kim could respond Reggie had closed the door.

"He's so gruff. Doesn't that bother you?" asked Kim. She had set her magazine down and was looking at the expiration dates of some canned goods. "This went bad in 1992," she exclaimed.

"Yeah, that's why you gotta rotate your stock," Nick joked, swirling his finger in a circle. "You don't have any idea who Reggie is, do you?"

"Should I?" Kim wondered as she came closer to Nick.

"Ever heard of Zulu Omega?" he asked.

"Sounds familiar," Kim responded as she tried to recall.

Nick made a fist and raised it into the air.

"Oh," she whispered.

Nick sat down on the cold, cement floor and began his tale.

The Virtue of Vices - Jeremy McShurley

Zulu Omega had been the leader of the Black Pumas, a local offshoot of the Black Panther Party, organized at Princemoore University. While never verified, rumor was they held meetings in the basement of Whispering Willie's, the building where Holidaze currently stood. Because of their small size, the Black Pumas coordinated with other revolutionary groups; staging war protests, vandalizing political headquarters, and providing shelter for draft dodgers on their way to Canada. They also stole food and clothing, and then redistributed it to the black community in the south part of the city and the poor whites west of the river.

The group's activities continued until the late seventies. As the young radicals grew weary of hiding from the law and living in squalor, Zulu disbanded the Black Pumas, proclaiming their movement had brought about social justice, women's rights, and ended the war in Vietnam. Zulu dropped the moniker. Reginald Holland then started focusing his time and efforts on his three daughters, the result of several short-term flings at Whispering Willie's commune during the Free Love Movement.

For the first time in his life, Reggie got himself a real job, working the line at Princemoore Transmission. But his heart hardened during the 1980s as he watched the economic and social progress he had championed get dismantled by the conservatives in Washington. When Princemoore Transmission was shipped south of the border after the signing of NAFTA, Reggie got a job washing dishes at one of the university's dormitories. His daughters had moved away years before and had children of their own, and he rarely spoke to their mothers. Reggie had retired a couple of years before Nick came to work for him. These days, he either watched old black and white movies or sat silently at his favorite coffee shop, reminiscing about his youth.

"What a life," Kim commented as Nick finished up.

"It took a while to get the details. I figured it out when I was going through his stuff and found an old chest filled with Black Puma paraphernalia. At first, he told me he didn't know where it came from. So, I did a little digging on the Internet and found out as much as a could. Every once in awhile I'd drop a little trivia, but screw it up on purpose. Eventually he cracked and yelled, 'Damnit, boy! You done got it all mixed up'."

Kim could imagine Reggie yelling in that wonderful Southern accent.

"He showed me his, so I decided to show him mine," Nick stated as his stood back up.

"Yours?" Kim inquired.

Nick smiled, and his grey eyes began to shine. He didn't give out his history often, but today seemed like the appropriate time.

"My uncle is former Congressman Doug Stone. My grandma is Gloria Stone. Granddaughter of Talia and Alexander Princemoore," he confessed.

"Holy moly," Kim gasped.

"Yeah. Imagine those family reunions," Nick touted with a hint of pride. "Once Reggie knew who I was he opened up. He knew I didn't have to work if I didn't want to. I told him I wasn't like everybody else. People like him. Those are my heroes. They're the one's who can really make a difference."

"That's crazy. I would have never guessed in a million years," Kim admitted, shocked to be in the presence of White River City royalty.

"I've been picking ole' Reggie's brain for the last six years. He's taught me a helluva lot more than anything I learned in class. And one day, I'll take up the Zulu mantle, and bring the Black Pumas back into the spotlight," Nick proclaimed with a seriousness in his voice Kim had yet to hear.

She gently touched Nick's cheek. "It's going to be sooner rather than later."

"Oh no," he replied, understanding her meaning. "How long?"

"Weeks? Maybe a couple months," she revealed.

Nick's lips started to tremble. His eyes became wet, and he tilted his head towards the heavens in silent prayer.

The emotional and physical fatigue from her twelve-hour shift became too much. She wrapped her arms around Nick's neck and starting crying with him. They shed tears, but not in sadness. Instead, Nick and Kim recognized the ever-present cycles of the universe, and that death comes to all of us, but life is something one must seek out themself.

The door burst open, "Boy! That soup ain't gonna cook itself," Reggie declared.

Nick and Kim's gently weeping transformed into a vibrant chuckle. Kim looked Reggie directly in the eyes, "He'll be right in, Zulu Omega."

Reggie's dour face transformed into a vengeful scowl, "Hope ya enjoyed your chat with Mr. Princemoore here," he hollered before slamming the door.

"Come on in," Nick offered. He showed Kim the rest of the house while Reggie sat silently in his worn out recliner and watched World War II movies. Stacked in the basement were television sets from throughout the decades. Upstairs were three bedrooms. Each contained plastic tubs that were filled with clothing for men, women, and children, and organized as such. Only the living room and kitchen remained free of clutter, and Kim imagined that Reggie must sleep in his chair or on the couch.

Nick finally made Reggie's soup. He asked if Reggie would join he and Kim at the kitchen table, but Reggie refused, preferring to eat alone in the living room. After the meal, Nick and Kim went outside to pick up the backyard. Nick told her the story of the time the Black Pumas had spray painted one of the dean's houses. They had to hide in the sewers for two days until the police stopped their search.

Nick and Kim then went back inside, cleaned up the kitchen, and said their goodbyes.

"Mr. Holland," Kim said, standing by the front door. "Thank you."

"I didn't do nothin'," the old curmudgeon responded.

"You've done more than most people will do in three lifetimes. It was an honor," she informed him as she stepped outside.

"You going up to the Beanstalk later?" Nick asked.

Reggie waved Nick off. "I'm still mad at you."

"Love you, Reg," Nick professed, closing the door behind him. He then walked Kim to her car.

"What's going to happen to all that junk?" Kim wondered aloud.

"Who knows? Maybe he'll let me use it for the Revolution," Nick guessed.

"Good luck with that," she responded as she got in her car.

The Virtue of Vices – Jeremy McShurley

"You wanna know why he did it, why he keeps everything?" asked Nick as he crouched to Kim's eye level.

Kim waited for Nick to explain.

"Reggie, well, Zulu Omega, spent most of his life trying to give to those who had nothing. He looked around and saw homes overflowing with useless and unused things. Four people living in a house big enough for ten. He tried to change the world. But the world wasn't ready for Zulu Omega. I guess one day he snapped. Started taking as much as he could. Said he was 'tryin' ta keep those damn fools from takin' everything.' But honestly, I think he just didn't know what else to do with his life."

"It was nice to meet you, Nick. Come see me next time you need a flu shot," Kim winked. She drove down Weaver Street, wondering if she was going to have the energy to go the Caleb Brown show later tonight. In the rearview mirror she saw Nick Stone; standing with his fist clenched and his arm raised as high as the sky.

**Indecency** - (*in-dee-suhn-see)*
Behavior that is obscene, improper, or outside of the standard social norms

> **Sir Devaleus:** !*Go north*
> *You enter a small glade. There is a path to the North and West. The sun shines through the trees casting shadows of the leaves on the muddy ground. A small chest sits at the trunk of one of the trees.*
> **Sir Devaleus:** !*Open chest*
> *The chest is locked.*
> **Sir Devaleus:** !*Break lock*
> *STR CHECK: 23*
> *You have unlocked the chest.*
> **Sir Devaleus:** !*Open chest*
> *You open the chest. Inside you find 20 gp, a rusty dagger, and a cloak.*
> **Sir Devaleus:** !*Take 20 gp !Take cloak*
> *ADD INVENTORY: 20 gp; cloak*

Dan noticed the face of his phone light up. He looked to see who was calling and saw it said *Mystical Dave.* He picked up the phone and answered it.

"Hello?"

"You finished with work yet?" Dave asked.

"Huh? Oh, yeah. Just got done. Sorry about earlier but you know how it goes," responded Dan.

"Not really. That's the great thing about being self-employed," Dave laughed.

"Weren't you were playing cards tonight?" Dan questioned as he stood up and stretched. He had left Dave and one of his co-workers in the middle of dinner a few hours ago, claiming to have an

## The Virtue of Vices – Jeremy McShurley

emergency at work. In reality, he had come home and logged into one of his online role-playing games.

"I was. Got taken to the cleaners pretty early. But I saved a few bucks for a little drinking. Feel like meeting up at Caligula's?" Dave asked.

Dan considered his options. He could stay at home alone and play games all evening. Or he could go to Caligula's Parlor and have stripper boobs shoved in his face all night. Either way, it would take his mind off of Gretchen. "Sure. What time?"

"I'd like to get there around nine before it starts getting real busy. Sound like a plan?" Dave wondered.

"Ok. I can do that. See you in a bit." Dan hung up the phone then saved the progress of his game. He still had his work clothes on and decided to wear just those instead of changing. Strippers like a guy in a suit. He then brushed his teeth and gargled some mouthwash. After that, he dumped a little bit of food into his cat's food dish and left his house.

Dan and Dave found a table just off the main stage. Caligula's Parlor opened at six but didn't really start hopping until ten or so. The bar closed down at three, but they didn't lock the doors until five in the morning, giving the girls a chance to make a little more money and the drunks some time to sober up. Dave got the attention of a server and ordered a couple of drinks. They came pretty quickly, and he and Dan turned their attention towards the lone dancer on stage. She was wearing nothing but a purple g-string and had a furry purple boa wrapped around her torso, covering her breasts. There were only a couple of guys up close watching her show, so she kept herself covered for the most part until money started getting tossed onto the stage.

"Oh, by the way, you owe me forty for dinner," Dave informed Dan.

Dan started reaching into his back pocket for his wallet. "Sorry about that."

Dave laughed, "I'm messing with you. Just buy me a couple of rounds, and we're square. Boy, that Gretchen, she is something else," he began.

"I don't want to talk about it," Dan interjected.

"She the one you been talking about?"

"I said I don't want to talk about it," Dan said more emphatically and turned back towards the stage, taking a long drink. He had come here so he wouldn't have think about her. Dan quickly downed the rest of his beverage then looked around for a server. Once he caught her eye he raised his glass and shook the ice around, indicating he wanted another.

Dave had barely touched his bourbon. He preferred to sip throughout the evening without getting too buzzed, as he was more of a public figure than his friend. Dave's younger brother, Tim, had introduced him to Dan years ago. Dan and Tim were classmates, and Dave had graduated high school several years before they were even freshmen. Opting to skip out on college, Dave moved to Estrada Beach to try to make it in show business. During his time between auditions and waiting for callbacks, he honed his skills as a magician. While acting was his first love, he had a knack for illusions and was able to pay the bills performing street magic on the Seagull Strip.

His reunion with Dan was a somber one as Tim had died in a car crash on prom night. The two grabbed a bottle of cheap vodka and Tim's golf clubs then snuck onto the Deerwood Hills golf course the night of the wake. Dave had never been very close with his brother when they were kids, and he plied Dan for stories about their adventures. They knocked golf balls around the course all night, taking swigs from the bottle, reminiscing, and crying together. That was the first time Dave had ever seen Dan shitfaced. Since then he rarely saw him have more than a couple. But it looked as though tonight might end up being an exception.

The server brought Dan's drink, and he handed her his credit card. "Could you open a tab for me, please?"

"No problem," she responded taking the card.

"And, go ahead and put his next couple of drinks on it, would you?" Dan requested.

The server nodded and went to check on some other tables.

"So, Vegas? When does that show start?" Dan asked.

"Really soon. I have those two gigs here next week. Then I'll be moving out there week after that. I'm just glad I'll be out there before Halloween. My Ghosts and Ghouls set is one of my favorites."

After Tim's death, Dave had moved back in with his parents. His mom didn't take the loss well at all, and Dave's father was too emotionally detached to be much help. Dave would go out on the road for a couple of weeks, then return to check on his mom's condition. After a mourning period of about a year, she returned to her former self, although still wrought with occasional bouts of melancholy. Dave ended up preferring the situation. White River City was much cheaper than the west coast, and it allowed him to add equipment and new tricks to his act much faster than before. He also was able to build up a large local fan base, as he was no longer a small fish in a big ocean.

As Dan and Dave chatted about their past experiences in Sin City, the club began filling up. The smaller stages in the corners now had dancers as well, and there were two girls on the main stage. The pace of the servers picked up too, as did Dan's drinking. After an hour Dave had noticed that Dan's speech was starting to slur a bit. Dan stopped a passing server to order another round.

"I'll take a Bloody Mary. No, a vodka tonic. No, I know. I'll have a tequila sunrise."

The server nodded and started to walk towards the bar. Dan reached out and grabbed her by the arm. "So, how's come you're not up there dancing? You got a great ass and nice big titties. You need to be shaking those things making the big bucks," he ended his statement by tossing a handful of dollar bills above her head.

She scowled and broke free, hurriedly walking away.

Dave put his hand on Dan's shoulder. "I think you should probably slow down."

"I think you should stop telling me how to live my life," he ended with a hiccup and a belch.

"You can't be grabbing the staff. They'll throw your ass out," Dave warned.

"How about if I let her grab my staff? My big, wizard staff," Dan said as he pantomimed an exaggerated size of his penis.

"You fucking wish," Dave retorted, shaking his head. He turned his attention to the main stage. The dancer to the front had her legs wrapped around the pole and was slowly pulling herself up towards the top. But it was the girl at the back that caught Dave's eye. He watched in amazement as she

## The Virtue of Vices – Jeremy McShurley

contorted her body like a snake, pulling her right leg up behind her neck while standing on her left tiptoes. She set her leg back down, went into a backbend and then a handstand. She finished the maneuver by rolling forward into the splits and leaning her chest just off the stage. The crowd went wild, and her white thong quickly filled with bills as more money showered the stage.

"I'll be right back," Dave told Dan. He got up and started to head towards the flexible dancer who was just coming down the steps. A few of the guys were still clapping and hooting, and she turned towards them and took a bow. He followed her as she made her way towards the dressing rooms.

"Nice moves," he said.

"I thought so too." The dancer was tight and fit with a beautiful face and streaked blonde hair.

"How much for a private show?" he inquired.

"How much ya got?" she quipped.

"I have a debit card, and you guys have an ATM," Dave explained.

"Meet me in Colosseum Room in five," she told him.

Dave smiled and turned to head back to the table. He hurried his gate when he saw Dan standing uncomfortably close to their server.

"How about I let you sit on my sword +8? As in eight inches," Dan wobbled a bit with his last sentence.

"Ok, that's it. You're done," the server proclaimed. She caught the attention of one of the bouncers, raised her hand in the air and pointed at Dan.

Dave got to Dan's side just as the bouncer arrived. He watched as the bouncer grabbed Dan by the arm and started pulling him towards the side exit. Dave followed just behind.

Dan started to struggle but was no match for the strength of the bouncer. "I'll cast fireball on your ass," he threatened.

The bouncer shoved Dan out the door, who then stumbled and fell onto his stomach. He turned over onto his back and pointed both fingers at the bouncer. "Pew pew. Lightning bolt. Pew pew."

Dave waited for the bouncer to go back inside before checking on Dan. He helped him sit up and brushed some dirt off his back. "Come on. I think it's time for a nap," Dave said as he pulled Dan to his feet.

"I was going to fuck the shit out of her. I was. I was going to break her soul," Dan kept rambling the entire way to Dave's car.

"Yeah. You were almost there, buddy," Dave placated him. He opened the car and helped Dan lay down in the back seat. Dave assumed that he was going to have to tell Dan about his little misadventure tomorrow. After a minute or so Dan was passed out. Dave rolled him onto his stomach and turned his head towards the side. He then bent Dan's legs and gently closed the door.

"I was about to give up on you," said the flexible stripper.

"My friend had a little incident. Glad you waited," Dave said thankfully.

There were four private rooms at Caligula's; the Forum, the Amphitheatre, the Temple, and the Colosseum. Each room had a large seat covered in velvet at the back and small marble statues placed throughout. But the murals on the walls were what differentiated each style. The Colosseum room's mural was of naked female gladiators fighting lions, bears, and each another.

"I'm Kameron by the way. Kameron Falls," she introduced herself. She took Dave by the arm and led him towards the velvet chair.

"I'm Dave," he said as he sat down.

Kameron stood in front of Dave silently waiting for him to pony up. He quickly took the hint and pulled out five crisp twenties fresh from the ATM. She graciously took them and then tucked them into the right strap of her thong. She then began to gyrate her hips back and forth and started to pull her short white t-shirt up over her head.

"Hold on, Kameron," Dave said just the bottom of her shirt had reached the top of her breasts.

She let her shirt fall back down. "You don't want a dance?" she asked quizzically.

"I'd be lying if I said I didn't want a dance. But really I just want to chat," Dave explained as he leaned forward.

Kameron became a little suspicious and nervous. She had never had a request like this before, and she had heard plenty of strange requests. She had started dancing five years ago at The Queen of Hearts across town. As in many cases, it was a job taken out of necessity. She had never considered trying to work at Caligula's, believing it out of her league. But one of the bouncers had spotted her act one night and brought her to meet Caligula's manager, Mason. He was impressed and started her out on the corner stages during the week. After a few months of hard work and dedication she finally got the opportunity to make her main stage debut tonight.

Kameron Falls was not her real name, of course, her given name being Michelle Cameron. Like a lot of the girls she had been born and bred in White River City. Kameron never had the opportunity to go to college. When she was a child, she thought she was going to be a gymnast. It was something she had been training for since she was ten years old. Growing up on the city's west side was tough. Her dad had lost his job when Princemoore Transmission moved to Mexico when she was only four. He had been living off of welfare and food stamps ever since. After her mom died from alcoholism a couple of years later, she felt like she had lost her family all together. But she got a new family in the form of the gymnastics team. When they weren't training, they would ride over to the other side of the river and look at the big mansions. She knew she would live there one day from all of her endorsements after winning gold at the Olympics.

After her high school came in second at state she thought her Olympic dreams might be starting to become a reality. But during tryouts, she snapped a ligament in her wrist on a failed vault attempt her sophomore year. The doctors told her it would heal, but she would never be one hundred percent again. When she came home in a cast, her dad took one look at her and said, "There goes that meal ticket." Those were the last words he ever spoke to her.

"Ok," Kameron said as she sat down cross-legged in front of Dave. "Chat about what?"

"This might sound a little weird," he began.

"Oh, it's already a little weird, Dave," she sarcastically replied.

"I'm going to be leaving town pretty soon, and I didn't want to miss the chance of talking with you. I've been doing stage magic for quite a few years, and I've wanted to take on a partner," he explained.

## The Virtue of Vices – Jeremy McShurley

"I don't know anything about magic," Kameron admitted, shrugging her shoulders.

Dave leaned in even closer, putting his nose an inch away from hers. "And I can't fold myself in half. There's a lot more money in a group act. I've tried it before with a couple of girls, but they don't have what you have. The things you can do with your body, it's amazing. I can teach you how to do the tricks, but I can't teach another magician how to contort. You wouldn't believe the ideas I got watching you tonight. I know what the audience in Vegas will want, and they're going to want you," he sat back as he finished.

"That is an interesting offer. How do I know you're not bullshitting me?" Kameron asked, still uncertain of Dave's authenticity.

"Come to my show next Wednesday. I'm playing the Carson Auditorium. If you like what you see, we'll put a couple of tricks together on Thursday and debut them the next day. Then, we can both go out to Vegas and give it a shot. If it doesn't work out, you'll always have a backup plan." Dave clasped his hands together and stared into Kameron's eyes.

She was mesmerized. The way he spoke to her made her feel inspired, something she hadn't experienced for a long time. He certainly seemed to have a special type of aura about him.

"Look, you're great at what you do," he said breaking the silence. "And I'm sure you can do this for another ten years and make great money. But, one day those tits are going to start sagging, and those legs of yours aren't going to bend like they do. Didn't you ever dream about something bigger? Something better than White River City?"

Kameron felt a lump in her throat. She barely knew Dave, and she certainly wasn't going to let him see her cry, at least not tonight. She swallowed and said, "The thought has crossed my mind."

Dave stood up and started walking towards the door. "Good. I'll see you Wednesday then."

"Wednesday. And just so you know, I'm keeping the money," she proclaimed.

"What money?" he asked eyeing her waist.

Kameron looked down at her thong. The five twenties were missing. "What the?"

When she looked back up she found herself staring at the door. Mystical Dave had vanished into thin air.

## The Virtue of Vices – Jeremy McShurley

**Jealousy** - *(jel-uh-see)*
Exhibiting signs of distrust or feelings of suspicion over the fidelity of one's partner

"Who is she, Grant? Who the fuck is she?" Maria Carroll shouted at her husband from across the living room.

"What the hell are you talking about?" he responded as he dried his hair, still damp from the shower.

Maria stomped across the room and showed Grant his phone. "Here," she pointed at a number from his call history. "This number. Right here. Who is this? They've been calling you the last two weeks. Are you too stupid to delete your whore's number?"

Grant tried to grab the phone from Maria's hand, but she quickly pulled it away and held it behind her back. He tossed the towel onto the nearby loveseat and took a deep breath. As a police officer, he was trained to de-escalate situations, but he always found it most difficult to handle the sudden, and as of lately more frequent, outbursts from his wife. The two had been married for seven years and had gone through rough patches in the past, but Maria's demeanor was beginning to become an issue. He silently stared at her, waiting for her posture to relax, and then made a quick swipe for his phone, pulling it out of her unsuspecting hand.

"This number?" he pointed. "I have no idea. It's probably some telemarketer. Look, it says it's from Estrada Beach. Who do I know from Estrada Beach?"

Maria tried to get the phone back, but Grant held it high above his head, jerking it back and forth from her attempts to grab at it. "Telemarketer? You expect me to believe that?"

"I don't know what else to say, Maria. You want me to block it?" he suggested.

Her silent stare appeared to be a yes.

"Here, look," Grant turned the face of the phone towards Maria. He pulled up his contacts list, selected the Estrada Beach number and started to press *Block* from the menu.

"Wait," she stopped him. "Call it. I want to hear the voice of that homewrecking slut."

"Call it? You want me to call some telemarketer? Great idea, Maria. That'll get me put on what, fifty other calling lists?" he tried to reason with her.

Maria plopped down on the couch and looked at her husband with a furrowed brow and pursed lips. "Call it," she commanded.

Grant shook his head and shrugged his shoulder, "Fine," he acquiesced. He pressed the *Call* button and waited for the phone to start ringing.

"Put it on speaker," Maria told him.

Grant did as she said and the sound of ringing filled the room. After four attempts the ringing stopped, and there was silence. After a few seconds, the speaker on the phone started making a succession of short, annoying beeps. "Happy?"

Maria stood up. "Oh, very clever. Your whores are getting smarter," she noted as she made her way towards the kitchen.

"What whores?!" Grant shouted as he kicked the coffee table onto its side, sending remotes, magazines, and coasters flying into the air. "Fuck!" Grant grabbed ahold of his barefoot and held it to try and stop the sharp pain. He pulled his hand away and noticed that the nail on his big toe had pulled up a bit and a small amount of blood had appeared under at the tip.

## The Virtue of Vices – Jeremy McShurley

He heard what sounded like Maria violently washing dishes in the kitchen and he gingerly walked into the bathroom, holding his right toes just off the ground. He scrounged through the closet looking for the adhesive bandages and pulled out a box that looked to be several years old. Grant flipped through the selection and pulled out the largest bandage he could find. He set his foot up on the sink and wrapped his big toe, wincing a bit.

Grant looked up into the mirror, his face still flushed with anger. He saw the reflection of his uniform hanging behind him. Grant had met Maria just out of the academy almost a decade ago. She was a cocktail waitress at the reception for his graduating class, and he had been eying her the whole night. Towards the end of the evening, with several drinks of liquid courage coursing through his veins, he asked for her number. She told him she wasn't allowed to give her number to event guests, so he waited in the parking lot for her to get off work.

"The party's over, so how about that number?" he smoothly asked.

"I think the party's just about to get started," she replied with a wink and a smile.

Maria was a natural beauty. She had long, straight, jet-black hair, dark eyes, and a smooth olive complexion courtesy of her father, Alonzo Huerta, a professor of Latin American cultural studies. Huerta had fled his native Nicaragua in 1982 during the conflict between the Sandinistas and Contras. Maria was born two years later while her father was teaching at Princemoore University. Although the political unrest had settled down by the mid-90's the Huertas decided to remain in White River City where they felt Maria would have more of an opportunity.

## The Virtue of Vices – Jeremy McShurley

Her parents sent her to the esteemed Hollowdale Academy, a private co-ed school located a few hours south of the city. Unlike her father, Maria was not the academic type and preferred staying up late and sneaking into the boy's dorms to party. By her junior year she had accrued enough demerits to garner a suspension that caused a great strain in her relationship with her family. She never returned to school, opting instead to get her GED when she was seventeen. While her parents were disappointed in her decision she never bothered them for money, instead taking any job she could find to pay the bills and continue her reckless lifestyle.

A couple of years later she made contact with some relatives in her family's native country and flew down to stay with them. It wasn't long before she started dating a small-time drug dealer named Renaldo who lavished her with fine dinners, jewelry, and expensive vacations. But the relationship lasted barely a year as one night a rival gang broke into their home and shot Renaldo right in front of her. As the assailants held a gun to her head, she pleaded with them, promising she wouldn't speak a word and would move back to the United States, vowing never to return. The gang's leader made a small cut into her left cheek as a reminder of her oath, and she was on a plane back home the next day.

Shortly after that, she met Grant. With the nightmares of her near-death experience still haunting her, dating a police officer seemed like the most logical decision. They saw each other off and on for a few years before Grant finally made it official, proposing to her on her 23rd birthday in front of friends and family. Grant had taken the traditional route of asking Professor Huerta for permission first. The family was overjoyed at the

# The Virtue of Vices – Jeremy McShurley

prospect, as Grant had managed to tame Maria's wild side, at least as best he could. They loved Grant, as he had proven to be an upstanding citizen both at home and on the force. Mrs. Huerta offered Grant her grandmother's engagement ring as a gift, and when he slipped it on Maria's finger on a gorgeous spring evening seven years ago, there wasn't a dry eye at the table.

Grant splashed water on his face as he began to calm down from the argument. As he brushed his teeth, he looked at himself in the mirror, wondering how someone like him ended up with someone like her. He wasn't unattractive, but he also wouldn't be gracing the covers of any magazines. Maria, on the other hand, could have been a model but instead wound up with a beat cop from Middle America. Although the fighting had been increasing, he still considered himself lucky to have her. All marriages go through periods like this, he thought. They would just have to ride it out.

After finishing cleaning up and putting on his uniform, he returned to his mess in the living room. He picked up the table and placed everything back on it. The door to their bedroom was shut, and when Grant went to open it, he noticed it was locked. He lightly tapped his index finger on the door. "You sleeping?" he asked. After an argument, Maria's typical response was to shut all the curtains, pull the covers over her head, and take a nap. He didn't hear an answer, so he continued, "I'm heading to work, ok?"

"I thought you didn't work until five. You going to visit your whore, let her know I'm onto her?" she shouted through the door.

Grant felt his anger swelling again and he shouted back, "Yep! That's it! We're gonna meet up at my secret fucking apartment, that I can totally afford, and fuck like rabbits! Jesus Christ. Have you thought about upping your meds?" Grant tried to bite his tongue, but it was too late. His last sentence hung in the air like fog on an early autumn morning. Maria had been on antidepressants during their first few years together. Only after gaining her complete trust and confidence did Grant manage to get the story of Renaldo out of her. She sobbed herself to sleep that night as Grant lay with her and held her until the sun came up. He convinced her to see a psychologist and try to get off the pills. The counseling ended up a success, and Maria hadn't taken any medication for the last five years.

"Babe," he lowered his voice. "I'm so sorry. I shouldn't have…"

"Go," she commanded.

"Just let me in for a…"

"I said go!" she screamed.

Grant turned and walked to the front door, grabbing his keys from a hook in the wall. He started walking towards his car then stopped and considered going back inside. He hated the idea of leaving Maria alone in their bedroom. Usually he could control his temper, but she had managed to get under his skin in an unusual fashion. Part of him felt as though she was pushing him away. As he thought back over the last few months, there were signs of Maria's suspicions. She had been questioning his whereabouts more and more often of which he explained away as having some drinks after work. He would also notice that his phone had been moved a few times but brushed it off. Despite what Maria believed, Grant was not having an affair. He had cheated on a girlfriend in high school many years ago at a party but the guilt he felt

The Virtue of Vices – Jeremy McShurley

stuck with him, and he vowed never to treat someone like that again.

He looked at the curtains of his bedroom window and again thought about trying to smooth things over before heading out for the day. Grant still had a couple of hours before coming on shift, and he never wanted to go to work without having told Maria that he loved her. His job was a dangerous one and, there was always a chance he wouldn't be coming home one day. He couldn't remember the last time he hadn't given her a kiss before leaving. But he also knew that Maria's present mood would make it difficult to work things out and he couldn't afford to be late. He'd be getting home well after midnight and figured Maria would already be in bed by then. So, he decided they would sit down and talk tomorrow. He started the car and drove off, hoping that work would take his mind off of things. Grant also said a little prayer as he wondered if his fat, piss poor excuse for a partner would end up setting off his emotions yet again.

After lying in bed for about twenty minutes, Maria got up, pulled the curtain back a bit, and peeked out the window. On occasion, Grant would leave something behind and she wanted to make sure he hadn't returned. Once certain he was gone for the day she began setting up her stage. She went into the closet and started pulling out her equipment. Maria first put up a frame around the bed that she had built out of tent poles, leaving the foot of the bed open. Then, she attached several large blankets to the frame covering the wall behind the bed and forming an enclosure to the sides. She then clipped two lamps to the frame and adjusted them to give the bed the appropriate lighting.

Next, she placed a TV dinner tray towards the foot of the bed and put her wireless webcam on top of it. Maria then rummaged through the nightstand on her side of the bed and pulled out an assortment of adult toys and lubricants. After that she changed into a blue, see-through negligee and a matching short silk lingerie robe. Maria finalized her outfit by changing her makeup, accentuating her already gorgeous features. Then she grabbed her laptop from the dresser, lay down on her stomach on the bed, opened up a private browsing window, and typed in a web address.

Maria had been a member of lonelyandhornycams.com for almost a year. Grant had been away at a seminar on community policing, and she was drunk and bored one night when she discovered the site. It started out as a joke, and at first, she only watched other user cams and partook in some minor self-fondling. But over the week that Grant was out of town she became more and more engrossed in the site, becoming familiar with several of the other camgirls and regular cyber-voyeurs. She learned that if she registered for an account, she could earn what were called Coins and later convert those into actual money. The day before Grant came home she spent five hours performing to 1000s of viewers. The night ended with an earth shattering climax and enough Coins to earn a couple hundred dollars. While she didn't end up telling Grant about her sexual adventures in cyberspace she did try to hint at the idea of doing a show together. He was either oblivious to or uninterested in her suggestions, and since that time Maria had become one of the website's most popular users.

She logged into her account.
**USERNAME:** *LatinGoddess94*

**PASSWORD:** \*\*\*\*\*\*\*\*\*\*

Maria usually spent the first few minutes chatting with some of her fellow camgirls. She briefly vented about her earlier argument with Grant and waiting for her viewers to begin showing up. Whenever she logged in an email notification was sent out to anyone who had *Followed* her profile. As her viewers slowly increased in numbers, she would chat with them either through typing or speaking into the webcam, normally about inane topics. On occasion, she would lean forward to expose the top of her breasts or switch positions on the bed to show off her panties under her robe. Once she reached enough users and the Coins started coming in, she began her show.

**LatinGoddess94**: *Hey there, HungTitan69. Haven't seen you in awhile.*

**HungTitan69:** *been 2 busy. I missed my Latin goddess*

**LatinGoddess94:** *too busy for me?*

**HungTitan69:** *I'll make it up to u*

HungTitan69 dropped 50 Coins into Maria's account.

"Wow," she said out loud. "You did miss me." Maria got up on her knees and slowly let her robe slip from her shoulders.

**mr_fister:** *Take it off. Let's see those titties!!!*

**HandSolo:** *I would so tear you in half*

**LordBoner42:** *show feet? Plz?*

Maria was used to this sort of banter and laughed it off. As the requests kept coming in, she lay back down and started typing.

**LatinGoddess94:** *Maybe less chatting and more Coin dropping boys...*

A few Coins came in but not enough for Maria to really get going. When she first started doing shows, she would end up naked and spent far too early. Over time she learned how to work her viewers for more and more Coins by slowing down her pace and teasing for longer periods of time. Maria had come to know her regulars and what it would take for them to drop Coins. A lot of the time she only had to gyrate in certain ways to please some viewers.

After an hour or so she had built her Coin total up to where she wanted it to be, at least for now. Normally she would put on several shows while Grant was at work, but she had planned on cutting this session a little shorter than usual. There was a big concert in town tonight, and Maria planned on meeting up with some friends and having drinks at a club called Holidaze later this evening.

She was finally completely naked, and the chat room's screen was moving too fast for her to keep up with all the messages. She shut the top of her computer and set it down on the floor. She then lay on her back, grabbed one of her toys and opened her legs towards the webcam.

"Don't worry, boys. There's enough of this to go around."

The Virtue of Vices – Jeremy McShurley

**Lust** - *(luhst)*
Feeling an intense and extreme sexual desire for someone or possibly something

      Members of the Princemoore Family had relocated to White River City during the natural gas boom of the late nineteenth century. Without the family's many contributions to the community White River City would be nothing more than a carbon-copy of every other farming town and village within an hour's drive. Mayor Jefferson Stone had convinced the Princemoores to buy a swath of land on the east side of the river to build a college. A few years later, Princemoore Memorial Hospital was constructed to handle the growing population. The family also funded the White River City Business Complex, a fifteen-story tower in the center of Downtown. After Raymond Princemoore was mysteriously murdered in 1972, his mother, Talia, had the building renamed in his honor.
      The Princemoore Building housed a number of small businesses and regional corporate headquarters. One of those was Princemoore Financial Partners, a diversified investment and real estate company that took up the entire twelfth floor. PFP had nearly gone bankrupt after making some ill-advised technology investments in the early 80's but a savvy new CEO named Frank Severstein was able to right the ship and has served at the helm ever since. Part of Severstein's strategy was to recruit heavily from Princemoore University in an attempt to slow the brain drain that normally accompanied graduation. Dan Preston was one of those hires, and he was currently in his fourth year of employment working for the Mergers and Acquisitions Department.

Dan was a typical workaholic, coming in early and leaving late on a weekly basis. His greasy hair, pockmarked face, and lack of fashion sense kept him behind the computer screen rather than leading meetings. But his ability to crunch numbers and foresee fiscal trends allowed him to begin his slow and steady ascent up the corporate ladder. He had recently been moved into a new office giving him a nice view of the Downtown cityscape. His office had also given him a view of one of the newer interns, an office assistant named Gretchen, whose cubicle was set just outside of Dan's doorway.

Gretchen was everything Dan was not. Her curly, strawberry blonde hair cascaded from her scalp to just past her shoulders. On the days she wore her hair up, Dan made note of the smooth nape of her neck and longed to run his fingers against it. She seemed to have an infinite supply of short dresses, skirts, and blouses always matching the colors of the season, and her high heels accentuated the firmness of her calves. Gretchen was outgoing, playful, and pleasant, sometimes to a fault. Her gregarious laughter made Dan's cheeks flush with excitement while her supple curves sent his blood flowing elsewhere.

On occasion, the two found themselves alone in the break room, and Dan would make attempts at inane conversation.

"A lot colder than normal, huh?"

"Oh, I know," she would respond.

From there, Gretchen continued the niceties while Dan's mind drifted. The thoughts of cold made him think of the effect it would have on her nipples. Her words moved into the background, and his fantasies took over, leaving him to stare blankly at Gretchen's plump, lipsticked lips. The tiny freckles

The Virtue of Vices – Jeremy McShurley

that started on her nose and curved down to her cheeks wriggled and wrinkled like stars dancing in the night sky. By the time the dryness in Dan's throat had passed, another employee had always entered the room.

"Nice, talking to you," Dan would finish, hastily leaving, usually without his lunch.

Time can be broken down into two concepts. There is the mathematical concept of time, that being $t = d/s$ and there is the concept of time as measured by the human mind. For instance, Dan had been calculating the amount of time it normally took Gretchen to finalize her end-of-day ritual and walk from her cubicle to the doors of the elevator down the hall. The commotion of Friday's employee weekend exodus was coming to an end, and only a couple of go-getters remained. Normally at the end of the week, Dan would stay until seven or eight, then round up some friends for a night of gaming and pizza. Dan had decided earlier in the week that today would be different.

Gretchen was almost always the last of the secretarial staff to leave. Before clocking out for the day, she would go over her work three times to ensure its accuracy. This was just another trait Dan found attractive, as most students her age were thinking about the weekend's adventures instead of Monday's paperwork. Dan understood there was a slight age difference between the two, but he reckoned her maturity in work ethic might balance out any chronological differences.

Dan had been planning his approach for the last couple of days and had stayed even later than normal throughout the week to get ahead on his projects. He could tell Gretchen was about finished as one of her last tasks was to make sure all the office equipment in her section had been either shut down or put into standby mode. She was over at the copy machine when Dan started stuffing some paperwork into his briefcase and then slowly walked over to grab his jacket from the coat rack. Just as he had calculated, Gretchen began to gather her things at 5:30 pm. He was about to step out the door when he heard a voice coming from the intercom on his desk.

"Preston, you still there?" He cursed under his breath as he heard the VP of his department calling for him.

He leaned over the desk and grabbed the phone. "I was just leaving, Mr. Addison."

"Really? I was wondering if you might be able to get me the Winchester loan numbers before you go?" Mr. Addison requested, oblivious to the stress in Dan's voice.

Dan looked up just in time to see Gretchen vanish out of view. "Actually, I have an appointment I have to get to. But I'll come in tomorrow morning and email them to you first thing."

There was a moment of silence as Mr. Addison contemplated. In the background, it sounded as though he was conferring with someone else. "That'll be fine, Preston. Have a great weekend."

"You too, sir." Dan's mind was racing as his entire plan was now off schedule. He wanted to sprint after Gretchen and initially started to do so, but he decided that would look unnatural. His goal had been to walk out the door at the same time in the hopes of giving rise to an off the cuff conversation. In his mind, he had run through several scenarios of what might be said and he was certain the mental practice would have allowed him to overcome the anxiety he usually felt in her presence. So instead of running, he briskly walked down the hallway towards the elevator lobby.

As he turned the corner towards the elevators, he saw the doors halfway closed. His voice caught in his throat as he tried to call out, "Hold the door!" Instead, he stared at himself in the mirrored facade of the elevator's exterior. He frantically pushed the down button hoping they would open back up. Instead, the display above the doors slowly changed from twelve to eleven.

$t=d/s$

Dan had ridden up and down those elevators more times than he could remember. He knew how slow they were, and that it was one of the morning's most common collective complaints. The stairwell stood only five feet from him, and he pulled the door open and began descending the staircase three to four steps at a time. If he could make each level in twenty seconds, he figured he could exit on the first floor just as Gretchen's elevator car was arriving. At the same time, he hoped other passengers leaving for the day as well might delay her ride.

He pushed on the bar lever on the first floor and rushed out of the stairwell while looking at the display on Gretchen's elevator. The number read five, and he stood there with a reddened face as he tried to catch his breath. While Dan managed to hold his own on the golf course, riding for miles in a golf cart did little to improve his anaerobic fitness. He leaned against the wall trying to look casual, shifting his position several times. Still, the elevator remained on the fifth floor.

Dan began to think he had miscalculated the elevator's speed. He started to assume that she had already exited and the elevator had gone back up for someone else. With a sigh of despair, he turned his back to the wall and leaned his head against it. Out of the corner of his eye, he saw the elevator's display begin to decrease. His heart started racing again, this time from nervousness. Dan ran his fingers through his hair and combed it as best he could. He pulled a breath mint from his jacket pocket and wiped the sweat from his hands, then bent over to pretend to tie his shoes.

The door opened, and Gretchen exited along with a couple of other people who Dan didn't recognize. He continued tying his shoes until the party had passed, then began to follow.

"Another day at the office, huh?" he awkwardly asked.

Gretchen turned towards the familiar voice, "Oh, hi, Dan. Yeah, another day," she agreed, smiling with a grin that went from ear to ear.

Dan's mind went blank. He had gone over his words a thousand times all week and yet again here he was dumbfounded and speechless. Gretchen had turned back around, and Dan's eyes fell towards the small slit that ran up the right side of her skirt. As her legs moved forward, it exposed the bottom of her hip, just below the panty line. He looked up and saw the building's exit less than thirty yards ahead. Soon the two of them would be in the parking lot, and it would be another weekend of Dan's imagination and lonely, late night Internet browsing.

Gulping down a ball of saliva, he moved forward to stand to Gretchen's left side.

"Do you like prime rib?"

"Excuse me?" Gretchen asked, confused.

"I was, well, what I was wondering," he stopped to collect his thoughts. "The Deerwood Hills Country Club has a really great prime rib. But it usually sells out really quick because it's so good, like I was saying. And, um. So, I know it's short notice, but if you'd like to come with me for dinner?"

"Actually, that sounds wonderful. I haven't had prime rib since I went to visit my parents."

"So, yes?" Dan asked, amazed at the answer.

"Sure. I'll follow."

Deerwood Hills Country Club was situated in the town of Santa Mesa just outside of White River City. Dan pulled into a crowded parking lot. Gretchen was close behind driving the hybrid her parents had loaned her while she was away at college. The two parked side by side then made their way into the clubhouse. The Deerwood Hills subdivision and its accompanying golf course were constructed in the 1980s. It was home to the affluent and influential, most of who worked in White River City. Dan's profession led to quite a few outings on the links, and he was a frequent visitor to the upscale community.

Dan was just about to ask the hostess for a table for two when he heard his name being called out from across the room. He turned to see one of his golfing buddies, a local magician named Dave Larson, vigorously waving him over. Already nervous about the situation, Dan thought he might be more comfortable with a familiar face in the mix.

"It looks like my friend already has a seat. Do you care if we join him?" he asked Gretchen.

"Three's company, right?" Gretchen agreed, shrugging her shoulders.

"And four's an orgy," Dan blurted out. He immediately wished he hadn't, realizing he wasn't hanging out with his gaming buddies. He half expected an email from HR on Monday.

"Um, sure," Gretchen replied, looking a bit uncomfortable.

Dan made a slight bow and extended his arm forward, "After you m'lady." He tried to imagine himself playing his *Ultimate Fantasy* RPG character, a paladin named Sir Devaleus.

Gretchen smiled and curtsied. "Why thank you, kind sir," she said, then proceeded towards their awaiting table.

Dan heaved a sigh of relief and decided to stay in character. He even pulled out Gretchen's chair for her as she sat and he took a seat next to her. "This is Gretchen, one of my co-workers," he explained to Dave.

Dave stood up and reached across the table to shake her hand, "A pleasure. I'm Dave."

"Good to meet you. So," Gretchen turned towards Dan, "Dan was telling me about the prime rib. I'm pretty excited."

"Best in a hundred miles," Dave concurred.

A server approached their table and introduced himself. He politely took everyone's orders and then repeated them back. "Bourbon on the rocks, vodka tonic with a twist, and three prime rib specials. Nothing to drink for you, ma'am?"

"Oh, no thank you. Not for a couple more years," Gretchen explained.

"Alright, thank you. I'll be back with your appetizers in just a few minutes," the server explained before moving to his next table.

"So what is it you do, Dave?" Gretchen asked as she initiated small talk.

"Ever heard of Mystical Dave?" he queried while making jazz hands.

"I thought you looked familiar. I've seen your posters around town. When's your next show?" Gretchen inquired.

"I have a couple coming up next week on Wednesday and then next Friday. Then, I'm off to Vegas! I'm doing a stint at the Paradisio Casino," Dave proudly announced.

"That's great, Dave," Dan congratulated him. "You really deserve it."

Their server set a basket of hot Italian bread on the table and a bowl of butter packets. "Just a couple more minutes on those apps," he assured them.

"Thank you," said Gretchen. "So, what's Vegas like? I've always wanted to go."

Dave leaned forward. "It's like nothing else in the world. The lights, the people, the constant bings and buzzing from the slot machines. You completely lose track of time. And walking across the street seems to take forever."

Dan had been to Las Vegas a couple of times as well. He tried to involve himself in the conversation, but Dave's bold personality almost always took over any discussion. He didn't do it on purpose, but as a stage performer for nearly his entire life, Dave's ability to work any crowd came as naturally as sunrise. Dan was elated when their dinners finally came as Dave's rambling was slowed down by the necessity to chew his food.

Gretchen smeared a large clump of horseradish onto her piece of prime rib and dipped it into the *Au Jus*. "Oh. My. God. You weren't lying, Dan. This is amazing. I could eat here every day. We have to tell everyone at work. Make it a regular Friday thing. Like Pizza Wednesdays." Gretchen then went back for several more pieces, moaning in culinary ecstasy with each bite.

Dan's mind drifted. Gretchen's sounds of pleasure set his imagination on fire. He could see himself gently nibbling all over her body, causing those noises himself. As the *Au Jus* dripped off of her fork, he began to think about Gretchen's own juices. The amount of room in his slacks slowly became smaller and smaller.

"Pardon me, Gretchen, Dave. I have to use the facilities," Dan announced, standing up with his napkin in front of his crotch. He turned around, dropped his napkin onto the table and made haste towards the men's bathroom. He prayed there was a stall available, and finding one, quickly entered and locked the door. He started thinking about anything but Gretchen; fire trucks, spreadsheets, eye surgery, the illegal ivory trade. Eventually, he managed to calm down his erotic urges. He turned around and urinated in case anyone had been in the men's room with him. He thought it might be strange for someone to stand alone in a stall for several minutes.

Dan opened the door and peered around but he was alone. He washed his hands and looked at himself in the mirror. "You are not Dan tonight. You, are Sir Devaleus. Protector of the Elven Kingdoms. Defender of truth and justice. Enemy of the Banesfolk! There is a princess who must be rescued from an evil sorcerer. Your mission is to finish your meal and escort Lady Gretchen to the movie of her choosing. For the Land of Wynsholm!" Dan ended his monolog by pretending to draw a sword from its sheath and then hold it high into the air. With renewed confidence, he turned and made his way back towards the table.

# The Virtue of Vices – Jeremy McShurley

He stopped just outside of the dining area. There were now two more individuals sitting at the table. One was a doctor he and Dave had joined on the course a few times. Dan could recognize the other person as well. It was one of the owners of his company, a terrible excuse for a human being and one of Dan's most sworn enemies. He had taken Dan's chair and had his arm around the back of Gretchen's seat. Sir Devaleus was about to charge in and slay the dragon, rescue the princess, and ride off into the sunset. Unfortunately, Dan had a mortgage, a car payment, and a ton of student debt to pay.

Dan walked up to the hostess stand. "I have an emergency at work. Could you let my friends over there know that I'll see them later? Thank you." He watched from the entrance as the hostess did as requested. Dave continued chatting while Gretchen looked around the restaurant.

"I will return for you some day, my beautiful princess, my goddess of love. My Scepter of Power shall soon be within your Sacred Chalice. But not tonight."

**Materialism** - *(muh-teer-ee-uh-liz-uhm)*
Focusing on value and possession rather than things of a spiritual nature

After saying their good-byes and collecting their winnings from the rest of the foursome, Peter Princemoore and Dr. Graham walked into the pro shop at the Deerwood Hills Country Club. Most of the golfers had started making their way back to the clubhouse as the sun was beginning its final descent for the evening. Peter and Dr. Graham had just finished a round of 18; pockets flush with new cash happily taken from their opponents. While not all golfers made wagers while playing, Peter and Dr. Graham had both the means and desire to bet on the outcome of each hole. Today had been quite a lucrative day for the two regulars players.

The two gentlemen turned in their scorecards and the key to the cart then stood around for a few minutes and chatted with some of the other players. As more golfers began to return to the clubhouse, Peter and Dr. Graham left the pro shop and walked into the attached restaurant, Gophers. Seeing that many of the seats had been taken, the two began walking towards the bar. Dr. Graham caught someone waving out of the corner of his eye and turned in that direction. He saw his friend, Dave, sitting across from a young, attractive redhead and diverted his course to their table with Peter in tow.

"Dave. You still coming over tonight?" the doctor asked.

"Wouldn't miss it for the world. Have a seat," Dave offered.

There were two seats available, although one had a half eaten plate sitting in front of it. Dr.

## The Virtue of Vices – Jeremy McShurley

Graham sat down in the chair with the empty plate setting while Peter took the other seat.

The redhead turned towards Peter. "I'm sorry, that seat's taken."

"Is it?" he wondered, sliding his chair closer to the young woman. "I'm Peter," he introduced himself.

"Gretchen," the redhead responded. "My friend just went to the restroom. He'll be back any second," she tried to explain.

Dave interrupted, "Gretchen, this is Dr. Graham." The doctor was wearing a neon green polo shirt and bright white trousers. He had a full head of light brown hair that was starting to grey just above the ears.

Gretchen turned and extended her hand to the doctor. "Nice to meet you."

"Gretchen works at Princemoore Financial Partners. I believe Peter is one of the guys who signs your paychecks," Dave informed her.

"Wait. Peter Princemoore?" Gretchen asked with wide eyes. She could now see the resemblance between Peter and the paintings of gentlemen that lined the wall at work. He shared the long, narrow nose of the Princemoore family along with their high cheekbones. Even the droop on the sides of the eyes was noticeable. But his hair was much lighter and starting to thin out.

Peter moved in even closer and put his arm around her chair. "That's right. So, I'll ask again. Is it?"

Gretchen found herself between a rock and a hard place as her co-worker, Dan, had invited her here. While she felt it would be rude to give up his seat, she also wanted to stay on the boss's good side. She looked over towards Dave for any suggestions, but he was engrossed in a conversation with Dr. Graham.

A female voice came from behind the party. "I'm sorry to interrupt. Your friend said he had an emergency at work and would see you later."

Gretchen began looking around for Dan, hoping to thank him for the invite.

"Well, that takes care of that," Peter exclaimed.

"That's a shame," Gretchen disappointedly stated. She turned towards Peter. "You should be proud. Dan really puts in a lot of time for the company."

"I'm sure he does." Peter grabbed Dan's unfinished meal and thrust it out in front of a passing server. "Here, get this out of here," he ordered.

Dave looked up at the server. "Can you box mine as well," he asked politely, pointed towards his plate.

"Of course," the server responded. She took the plate from Peter then walked around the table and picked up Dave's food as well.

"You taking off?" asked the doctor.

"Yeah, I wanna run home before the game," Dave explained. "Same time as usual?"

"Uh huh," Dr. Graham concurred. As Dave began gathering his belongings, the doctor looked over towards Gretchen, "What is you do at PFP?" he inquired.

"I'm Mr. Conner's personal assistant. Do you work at the hospital?" Gretchen asked, being well versed in small talk.

"I do. Are you a student?"

"Sophomore. I still haven't picked a major, though," she mentioned, a bit embarrassed. "I'm thinking about social services. But I still have a little time to figure it out."

"Social services?" Peter snidely remarked. "You might as well join a convent." With that statement, he stood up and made his way to the bar.

Dave was standing behind his chair waiting for his leftovers. He came around the table and stood next to Gretchen. "Don't mind him. He just acts like that cuz he never got a whoopin' growing up." He looked over to the doctor. "Nanny didn't wanna callus her hand," Dave joked with a grin spread across his jovial face.

Dr. Graham laughed as well, and even Gretchen smiled slightly.

The server returned holding a plastic bag. "Here you are, sir. Would you like this put on your account?" she asked.

"Yeah. I'll take care of the whole thing. Larson-7983," he responded. He then handed her a twenty and two fives.

"Thank you. Have a wonderful evening," she said.

"You too. Gretchen, a pleasure," he bowed.

Gretchen began digging into her purse. "How much do I owe you?"

"Don't worry about it. I plan on getting it all back tonight," he predicted with a wink towards the doctor. "Au revoir." Dave spun on his heels and casually headed towards the exit.

"I should probably get going too. Maybe I'll head up to work and see if Dan needs anything," she announced.

"No, please stay. I don't think we'll be here much longer," the doctor offered.

"Yes, stay," stated Peter, returning with a tray of four drinks. "Manhattans all around." He set the glasses down in front of all four seats.

"Oh, I can't. Two more years," Gretchen explained, gently pushing the beverage towards the center of the table.

Peter picked it up and set it back in front of her. "No one is going to card you with me around."

The Princemoores were White River City's wealthiest family. Other than the Stones, no one came close to their amount of power and influence. Peter's great-grandfather was Morris Princemoore, founder of the Santa Mesa line. Morris's brother, Alexander, had received the family manor, Tymborlyn when their father, Abraham, passed away. Morris took his inheritance and built his own estate, Umberland Fields, several miles north of White River City. While Alexander focused on the family's traditional investments, Morris began acquiring large swaths of farmland. In a few short years, he had built an agricultural empire, providing a variety of crops throughout the region.

During the suburban boom of the 50s, Morris capitalized on his landholdings, selling off a good portion of the surrounding property to developers, and reinvesting that money into the stock market. By the 1960's the area had grown enough in population to incorporate as the town of Santa Mesa. The town slowly expanded south towards White River City as the last, great generation of independent farmers were laid to rest in the soil of their forefathers, and the land was gobbled up by real estate and construction companies.

Peter's father, Karl, Jr., owned Princemoore Builders, and was a majority shareholder in Princemoore Financial Partners as well. While Peter was technically a vice-president in both companies, the title was more symbolic than functional. Like many of White River City's upper class, Peter had attended Hollowdale Academy, where he excelled at rugby and rowing. He was not, however, a studious academic. So when he wanted to follow his girlfriend to Forsyth University, his father had to pull more than a few strings.

By Peter's third senior year, Karl, Jr. threatened to cut him off if he didn't graduate. Burying his head in the books, Peter managed to finish second to last in his class. His girlfriend had graduated on time and was living on the east coast, working as a fashion consultant. When he discovered she had been secretly dating an actor, he beat the young thespian to the doorstep of death. The family had to pay a huge settlement, and Peter was sent to handle the Princemoores' affairs in Africa, where he spent his time big game hunting and sightseeing ancient ruins.

Once the media frenzy had died down, Peter returned home and took up his current position. He was rarely at the office, as most of his activities involved schmoozing with local politicians and executives on the golf course or at the tennis court. He even had a table reserved at Caligula's Parlor, an upscale gentleman's club just south of Santa Mesa. He could be charming when he needed to be, and it was his ability to finalize backroom deals that kept him in his father's graces.

"Don't pressure the girl, Pete," Dr. Graham said, coming to Gretchen's rescue. "Dave took off already, so that leaves two drinks for us," he suggested, taking Gretchen's from in front of her and sliding the fourth towards Peter.

Peter downed his original glass and then picked up the one intended for Dave. "You should really learn to take advantage of your situations, Gretchen. It's the only way to get ahead."

"I'm not really interested in getting ahead. I just feel blessed with what I already have," she replied.

"You had said you were a personal assistant. Is that part-time?" asked the doctor.

"Actually, it's a full-time internship. It ends at the end of the semester, but I'm hoping to stay on after winter break. I really like the people there," Gretchen explained, picking at her prime rib that had become cold.

"That's impressive," the doctor noted. "Full-time and going to school. I thought most kids your age just flipped burgers or slung espressos."

"I usually work full-time. It's part of the deal," she told him.

"Deal?" asked Peter.

"My parents let me use one of the cars while I'm in class. They also pay for my rent. But, I have to pay for half my tuition. Too poor to pay for it all, not poor enough to get any grants," Gretchen concluded.

Gretchen's family was from the southern part of the state. That area was much less populated and far more rural than White River City. Her mother made some extra money babysitting while her father had been working in a canning facility since after high school. For a long time, the family made a decent living. The union kept the wages up and the benefits coming. But the Great Recession took its toll, and a Chinese corporation called Long Feng Capital purchased the plant. To keep their jobs they had to scrap the union. Doing so cut the worker's paychecks in half and most had to give up their insurance plan and 401k.

What Gretchen lacked in book smarts she made up for in common sense. It wasn't that she couldn't grasp complex concepts. She was simply more concerned with the well being of others, a lesson instilled in her from her parents and her minister. Gretchen had been very active in her hometown church, teaching Sunday school, running the grill at the Fourth of July celebration, and volunteering to read scripture for the elderly at the nursing home. The members of her congregation had saved up to pay for her weekend trip to Princemoore University while she looked for a college to attend. She fell in love with the architecture and landscaping right away. When she returned home, she threw out all her other applications and put one hundred percent of her efforts into getting accepted and becoming a Puma.

"You know, if I remember correctly, there are a couple of Princemoore scholarships available," Dr. Graham mentioned, looking directly at Peter.

Peter shrugged his shoulders. The doctor tilted his head towards Gretchen who was again staring down at her plate. Peter finally took the hint.

"Yeah," he started, looking at Gretchen. "There are…"

Dr. Graham subtly placed three fingers on the table.

"…three. Scholarships?" Peter concluded.

Gretchen excitedly looked up. "Really? I've been looking online for grants, loans and scholarships for two years. I just can't find anything I qualify for."

"Well," Peter began, still not sure what the doctor was talking about. "You're in luck. Because. I happen to know the. Committee members," he faltered.

Dr. Graham put his hand over his mouth to hide his smile as he watched Peter squirm. The doctor wasn't so much a prankster as he was a scientist. He found the dichotomy between the two people sitting next to him fascinating, and he wanted to observe their interactions all night. But he had a poker night to host in a little while, so he was trying his best to see how Peter would manage to get his rich, pompous ass out of this situation. The doctor just continued to nod as Peter rambled on.

"It's a very complicated process," he began again after gathering his thoughts. "There are formalities to go over. And then, of course, there's the testing. Not to mention the physical examination. We'd need to see references..."

"Ok. I'll do it," Gretchen loudly pronounced, getting a few other guests to turn towards the table. "Whatever it takes, Peter. I need to go call my mom," she stated, leaning over to hug him. "Thank you, thank you, thank you. Just, email me the information. It's hoover.gc@princemoore.edu." Gretchen squealed with delight as she jumped up from the table. She could be heard telling her mom the good news as she exited the clubhouse.

Peter downed his second Manhattan, then reached across the table and drank one of the doctor's as well. "What? The fuck? Was that?" he asked as his volume gradually increased.

"It must be the whiskey talking," Dr. Graham lied, having barely touched his drink.

"I don't know anything about any scholarships," Peter confessed. "Is that even a thing?"

"Maybe. It sounds like something your family would do. Maybe you should start going to a few more meetings and stop chasing so much pussy," Dr. Graham suggested, taking a sip from his drink.

Peter shook his head in frustration, still fuming.

"Were you even listening to anything that girl had to say?" Dr. Graham asked.

"No," Peter admitted.

"She's not like us. She actually has to survive. Do you know what I do, Peter?" the doctor asked.

"Sort of. Doctor stuff," Peter generically answered.

"I heal people, at least I'm supposed to. I took an oath to do no harm. But sometimes I don't even know what that means. Sure, I can diagnose diseases, write prescriptions, and tell people not to smoke and to exercise three times a week. And I get paid a shit ton of money to do that," he began.

"That's good," Peter noted.

"Is it?" the doctor questioned. "Yeah, I'm making a ton of money. And you're loaded, and I still don't know what the hell you do. But most of these people. Maybe not 'these people,'" he said glancing around the room. "But most of the people out there in the world. They're just trying to get by. One fall down the stairs. One bad allergic reaction. One terrible phone call that the tests came back positive. That can destroy an entire family, wipe a savings account clean. Sure, I heal people, but at what cost?" Dr. Graham finished his speech then finished his drink.

"That. Sucks, I guess. To be those people. Not really my problem, though," Peter responded, still not quite understanding the doctor's intentions.

Dr. Graham stood up. "There may not be a Princemoore Family scholarship right now. But there could be, if you know what I'm saying," he said, head tilted down and looking through the tops of his glasses directly at Peter.

Peter sat there in silence for a minute. Then, he started a slow and quiet chuckle that quickly turned into a full-blown laughing fit, tears and all. "Oh, shit, Doc. You had me going there for a minute. You're almost as funny as Dave. Start a scholarship. Fuck that."

Peter continued to laugh as Dr. Graham left his golf partner for home. Behind him, he heard what sounded like a smacking sound.

"Hey, sweet cheeks. How about another round when you get a sec?" Peter ordered.

The doctor shook his head and pursed his lips. Some people just didn't want to be healed.

The Virtue of Vices – Jeremy McShurley

**Narcissism** - *(nahr-suh-siz-em)*
Psychological desire to be the center of attention often at the expense of others

The cool, fresh air was a relief as Josh Young stepped onto the front patio at Holidaze. His ears were ringing from the music that had been blasting in his face for the last couple of hours. Most of the crowd was still inside, but there were a few people out there with him; smoking, drinking, chatting, or just getting away from the sardine-like feeling of the packed music hall. His girlfriend, Kim, had never made it to the show. He imagined she had fallen asleep on the couch watching re-runs, and the thought caused him to yawn. He stretched his arms up into the air, realizing that Friday night had become Saturday morning an hour ago. Josh was exhausted, and the beer he held in his hand wasn't doing him any favors.

The doors to the music hall opened and the sounds of electronic dance music came blaring out, along with a couple of college students from Princemoore University. He nodded at them as they walked passed, but their attention appeared to be on the next destination. Several more groups of people started to leave, and he realized these must be Caleb Brown fans. His band's set had wrapped up just after midnight, and the post-show dance music didn't seem to have captured their interest. Josh had lucked out earlier when a parking spot became available just as he pulled into the lot. Instead of walking blocks to the nearest meter, he just had to head around back to get to his car.

He had been up for almost twenty-four hours, and he was starting to feel a little slaphappy. So, he decided to finish the rest of his drink and then go over to Kim's to snuggle with her. The two outside trashcans were overflowing with beer bottles and plastic cups, and he glanced around for a place to throw his trash away.

"Just leave it on a table," one of the bouncers instructed.

"Thanks," he responded, setting it down, then waving at the bouncer as he left the patio.

Josh walked a short distance down Main Street and turned right to head up Van Buren towards the lot. It had started to thin out a bit, as Main Street would be closing down in a couple of hours. He could see the band's caravan just ahead, consisting of a tour bus and a full sized RV. Josh laughed a little to himself. Caleb Brown was only a few years older than Josh, yet here he was traveling around the country in a house on wheels. He stopped and compared his 2001 Hatsuru compact to the behemoth of a vehicle only a few short yards away. The side was painted with the scene of a man battling a dragon. Josh had just put his key into the lock when he heard someone call out.

"Help," shouted a pretty blonde, wearing tight fitting jeans and a long, black flowing blouse. She ran up to Josh and grabbed him by the wrists.

Upon closer inspection, Josh noticed she had Indian tribal paint on parts of her face.

"Help me. He's not breathing," the girl pleaded.

"Who?" Josh asked, switching into paramedic mode.

"Caleb," she explained.

The painted girl pulled Josh along with unusual strength and led him into the RV. He did a quick survey of the scene. A flat screen television was playing what appeared to be a video from a

## The Virtue of Vices – Jeremy McShurley

Caleb Brown and the Skunk Munkies show. On the kitchenette table sat several bottles of half finished liquor surrounded by a few cans of beer and soda. The air smelled like pot and incense. Two small hand drums were sitting on the couch, along with a peace pipe and a deerskin pouch.

"He's back here. Quick," the girl informed Josh.

Josh followed her into the bedroom area. He saw Caleb Brown sprawled out on his back, wearing nothing but a beaded loincloth and covered in face paint similar to the girl. Josh pulled out his phone and started dialing 911.

"No!" the girl screamed and knocked the phone out of his hand.

"What the?" Josh asked in shock. "We need to call an ambulance," he demanded.

"No. Absolutely not," she firmly replied.

Josh climbed onto the bed and felt for a pulse. "This man needs medical care. Immediately," he tried to reason with her.

The painted girl climbed on the bed and reached over Caleb's body to grab Josh by the shoulders. She looked him dead in the eyes, "My dad is Detective Tranche. Do you know who that is?"

Josh silently nodded. Everyone in White River City had heard of Detective Tranche.

"If he finds out that I was here, doing drugs with Caleb, he will kill me. Then, he will get a voodoo priestess, to bring me back to life, and kill me again," she explained with pupils as large as saucers.

Josh surmised that she was on some sort of hallucinogen. At the same time, she appeared to have her wits about her. He felt torn. If he didn't call EMS and Caleb died, it would be on his hands. Yet, if he didn't listen to Detective Tranche's daughter, he would have an enemy for life. Again he checked Caleb's vital signs, shaking his head.

"Here, help me get him onto the floor. Um?" he prompted for the girl's name.

"Amanda," she responded.

"Ok, Amanda. Here, grab his feet," Josh commanded. He got at the head of the bed and lifted Caleb by the torso while Amanda dragged him off the bed.

"I can't believe this is happening," she noted, putting her hands over her nose and mouth. "Please don't die. It's not your time. Please. Don't leave."

Josh got on his knees and began performing compressions. "Now, Amanda. I need you to tell me exactly what happened."

Amanda continued to shake her head back and forth, mumbling under her breath.

Josh plugged Caleb's nose and blew into his mouth. He looked up. "Amanda!"

"So, this is Nick," Amanda's friend Brittany said, introducing the handsome young man with black hair and dark grey eyes standing next to her.

"Yeah, hey," Amanda responded, head turned away towards the stage.

"We're going to head out now," Brittany told her.

"Yeah, that's great," replied Amanda, still disinterested. She walked away, leaving Brittany and Nick in the bar area and began pushing through the crowd. Caleb's show had ended a few minutes ago, and the dance music had started pulsing through the venue. Amanda looked down at her phone, hoping to see a message, but there were none. She attempted to get backstage but was stopped by one of the bouncers. The roadies were in the midst of unloading gear from the stage.

Disappointed, Amanda headed back to the bar, ignoring a couple of guys she had been dancing with earlier in the evening. She briefly looked around for Brittany, then made her way toward the crowd that surrounded the bar. Amanda shoved her way through two layers of awaiting patrons, and then leaned towards one of the bartenders.

"Dylan! Whiskey sour!" she ordered, yelling over the music.

Dylan stopped what he was doing and made Amanda's drink, getting several annoyed looks in the process. She grabbed a hold of it and raised it up above the heads of the crowd, then started dancing her way back towards the stage again. Once there, she began to climb up, only to be stopped by a sound tech.

"You can't be up here," he informed her with a stern look.

Amanda tried several times to move around the tech, but he kept preventing her from climbing. She pouted, and finally gave up, then joined the rest of the crowd on the dance floor. Amanda felt her back pocket start to vibrate, and she quickly reached back and pulled out her phone.

**Unknown Caller:** *Come backstage. Show them this message.*

Amanda jumped into the air, sending her drink flying all over the crowd. She ignored the slew of curses that followed and ran to the backstage. Again a bouncer stopped her progress.

"I have a pass," she proclaimed, holding the face of her phone up to the bouncers nose.

The bouncer tilted his head back and read the message. "Go on," he said, letting her by.

The backstage area was dark except for a dim floodlight that showed the outlines of a few people and some equipment. The back door was open, and she could smell cigarette smoke wafting in. "Caleb," she called out.

"Are you the chic with the bra?" asked an overweight man with slicked back hair.

"That's me," she responded, shimmying her waist back and forth.

"He's downstairs," the man replied.

Amanda knew he was referring to the green room. It was the private area where bands could hang out before and after the show. Amanda had been down there a few times, but never with an act this famous. Again a bouncer at the door stopped her and again she showed him the text message. She called out Caleb's name as she descended the stairway.

The green room had seven occupants. Four she recognized as members of the band. The other three were apparently groupies, and they were down here for the very same reason Amanda was. Caleb was sitting alone towards the back on a burnt orange loveseat that looked like it was from the 1970s. He held her bra out towards her.

"I think you dropped this," he said.

"No, I threw it. I wasn't sure if you'd find the number." Amanda slowly walked over to join him on the loveseat.

Caleb scooted over and gave her room to sit. "I like your style. You don't think like everyone else," he told her in a delicate, wispy tone.

"That's what I always tell everyone," Amanda agreed. "I'm very unique. I know you like unique because I've read everything about you. I know your favorite color is love, that you like to vacation in the desert, and you have three cats;

named Brahma, Vishnu, and Shiva," Amanda rambled, and her speed picked up with every word.

Caleb set Amanda's bra off to the side. He turned towards her and ran his hand through her hair. "Your aura is very red and orange. But I see it is tainted with brown and black. I can cleanse you if you like."

Amanda wasn't exactly sure what Caleb was talking about, but she knew it would probably mean a trip to his RV, *Beowulf.* "Ok," she answered with a smile as big as a crescent moon.

Caleb led Amanda into *Beowulf.* He walked into the kitchenette and offered her a drink.

"Yeah," Amanda replied, looking around the interior. "Is that part of the cleansing?"

He poured a decent amount of whiskey into two glasses then topped them off with a can of open soda. "The body is an amazing piece of machinery. When properly tuned, it can fight off any and all disease. But, you must train the body to resist the poisons of the world. We drink to make the liver stronger," he raised his glass and downed the entire beverage.

Amanda followed suit, choking a bit.

Caleb grabbed a long, Indian peace pipe from the couch and stood before Amanda. He lit the pipe and inhaled deeply, then turned the pipe around and placed it into her mouth. "The whiskey has activated your solar plexus chakra. Now you must activate your third eye," he explained as he slowly blew marijuana smoke into Amanda's face.

Amanda took a small puff from the pipe and started coughing immediately. She felt the entire night's pool of liquor begin to rumble in her stomach. "Um hum," she said, lips pressed tight. "Be right back," she noted through clenched teeth. Amanda dashed towards what she assumed was the bathroom. Seeing that it was, she shut the door behind her, opened the toilet lid, and began purging several hours of whiskey sours, long island iced teas, vodka cranberry juices, and pineapple flavored malt beverages.

After heaving for several minutes, Amanda stood up and looked at herself in the mirror. Her makeup had been ruined from the tears streaming out of her eyes and the snot smearing across her cheeks. She turned on the sink and rubbed her face clean, drying it off with a nearby towel. She then wiped the rim of the toilet, flushed her vomit down, washed her hands, and returned to Caleb.

Caleb had changed into a colorful loincloth, covered in an assortment of beads and strings. He was sitting in the middle of the floor with two hand drums in front of him. "Sit, now that you are purged."

Amanda did as requested. "I'm very sorry about that. I never get sick. I'm kind of a badass."

"It is part of the cleansing journey. Join me," Caleb started playing a rhythm on the drums. Amanda tried to play along, but she didn't have the coordination to match Caleb's beats. He reached over and pulled a pouch off the couch. He then retrieved several different tubes. Caleb started chanting, and as he did so, leaned forward and began applying different colors of paint to Amanda's face. He set the paints down and began to drum again.

"Now, you must paint me," he commanded.

Amanda felt much more comfortable doing this, relieved to end her drum session.

"Do you know how old I am, Amanda?" Caleb asked.

"Of course. Twenty-seven," she answered as she continued to paint.

The Virtue of Vices – Jeremy McShurley

"Yes. There are some of us who leave this world sooner than others. Johnson, Joplin, Morrison, Hendrix, Cobain, Winehouse. Their spirit became so strong that the body could no longer contain it." Amanda finished her face painting, and Caleb stood up. He grabbed a remote and turned on the television. A video of the band was playing.

"Do you know why I make music?" he asked as he walked towards the kitchenette sink. He pulled a mortar and pestle from a cabinet, along with a small cloth bag.

"I read that you want to leave something behind," Amanda paraphrased from an article she had read.

Caleb grabbed a coffee mug from out of the sink and filled it with water. He then put it in the microwave and started to heat it.

"Yes. We must all leave something behind. Something that is not of the flesh. My spirit has come here to bring a message through song. It is why I am here and why I am adored. For my spirit has come before, and it will come again." The microwave beeped and Caleb pulled the mug out. Steam could be seen coming off the top.

"Come. We must now open your crown chakra," he explained as he led Amanda to the back room.

Caleb sat down cross-legged and invited Amanda to do the same. He set the mug of water off to the side, then dumped the contents of the cloth bag into the mortar. He used the pestle to grind the ingredients, and dumped them into the mug.

"This is called shoshowanu-tokowatok. It is a blend of herbs and plants that frees the mind of its mortal prison. The recipe was given to me by an old Indian medicine woman." He held the mug out towards Amanda. "It is the final step in your aura cleansing."

Amanda reluctantly took the concoction in her hand. It smelled like burnt leaves and rotten cabbage. She took a small sip then quickly passed it back.

Caleb took a drink as well, and the two passed the mug back and forth until it was gone. After a couple of minutes, Amanda spoke up,

"I'm not feeling… any...thing… wow." Her head tilted back and a myriad of geometric shapes appeared in her vision. Within each shape appeared a cluster of galaxies. The shapes began moving around randomly until they smashed together in the center, forming a dodecahedron filled with stars. She began to feel as though she was flying into the middle of the dodecahedron and the stars became brighter and closer until she was flying towards a single star. She then noticed a planet orbiting the star and began to approach it. It was a beautiful blue and green world much like her own. She dropped into the atmosphere and flew down out of the clouds. Below were trees, lakes, and furry creatures that looked like living, breathing stuffed animals from her childhood.

Amanda flew over the tops of herds of these creatures as they frolicked about, surrounded by sparkling lights and shimmering strands of gold. She approached closer and closer, eventually flying into the insides of one of the furry animals. She could see its internal organs and watched as its heart beat, and its lungs inhaled the fresh air. She continued to go smaller and smaller, first into the veins, then into the blood cells, and finally down to the atomic level. As Amanda approached the spinning electrons she realized that she was in yet another galaxy. Again she approached another planet, this one with new types of creatures. And again she went into their bodies, emerging in another world. This process repeated for what felt like hours.

Eventually, her vision began to clear, and she found herself laying on her side on the bed, drool coming out of her mouth. Caleb too lay on the bed as well. Amanda rolled over to tell him all about her beautiful adventure. That's when she noticed he had stopped breathing.

Josh pulled back from Caleb's mouth after his last blow. "It's not working. Amanda, I know you don't want to get in trouble. But he is going to die if we don't call for help."

Amanda imagined the look on her father's face when he found out. She saw him walking away from her, never to speak her name again. She saw herself sitting in a prison cell, wasting her life away. Then she saw the paramedics rushing into the RV. She watched them put paddles to Caleb's chest. She watched as he sat up and held her, and thanked her for saving his life.

"Ok," Amanda said on the verge of crying. She stood up straight and fought back the tears. "Do it. Call them," she finished by looking down at Caleb's lifeless, painted face.

Josh pulled his phone out. He pressed 911 and started to dial.

Suddenly Caleb began coughing. Josh dropped the phone and turned him on his side. A small bit of brown-red liquid dribbled out his nose.

"Oh, Caleb," Amanda shouted. She knelt down beside him and took his hands. "I thought we had lost you."

Josh put his phone back into his pocket. He went to the front of the RV and returned shortly with a glass of water, which he handed to Caleb.

Caleb was now sitting up against the foot of the bed. He graciously took the glass and gently sipped it. "Did I die?" he asked, looking towards Josh.

"In my expert opinion. You were dead there for a hot minute," Josh responded. "Do you want me to call an ambulance?" he asked.

Both he and Amanda shouted in unison, "No!"

"In that case, my work here is done. If anyone asks, I was never here," Josh requested, then left without another word.

"I thought you were gone," Amanda said, gently brushing her hand against Caleb's cheek. She was about to say that she never thought she'd see him again, but instead said, "I thought you'd never be able to write another song."

Caleb blinked and smiled. "Your aura. It has been cleansed."

The Virtue of Vices – Jeremy McShurley

**Obstinacy** - (*ob-stuh-nuh-see*)
Unwillingness to change one's opinion or give into the persuasion of others

   The basement floor cafeteria at Princemoore Memorial Hospital was relatively quiet, just the way Josh Young liked it. It was about an hour before the seven a.m. shift change, and most of the staff would either be finishing up their rounds or rushing through the final checklist of their daily paperwork routine. Josh had only been working at the hospital for a few months, but it hadn't taken him long to figure out how to maneuver through the chaos of the food court. After an initial couple of days of long lines and cold grub he decided it was best to beat the crowd rather than be beaten by it. Behind the register he noticed Sally, a lunch lady relic who people joked came with the building, and gave her a silent nod and a smile as he made his way towards the buffet.
   Each pan of food was still hot and steaming, leaving a coating of moisture on the underside of the sneeze shield. It was Friday, and that meant biscuits and gravy, Josh's favorite. He grabbed two biscuits with a pair of tongs and split each one in half, nudging them towards the top of the plate. He then ladled on two spoonfuls of what his mother would describe as "awesomey-goodness". He was tempted to add a third but remembered he was trying to lose a couple of pounds. Although, that didn't stop him from completing his meal with a scoop of scrambled eggs, three strips of bacon, and a slice of whole-wheat toast. At the drink station, he filled a large styrofoam cup with piping hot coffee and a smaller one with what was labeled as "orange juice", but Josh instead referred to it as "orange drink" for its lack of pulp and, more likely than not, vitamins.

The Virtue of Vices – Jeremy McShurley

There were only a couple of people ahead of him in the payment line, far fewer than his first few encounters with hungry hospital staff. It was hard to tell if they were coming on or leaving for the day. The appearance of early morning wakelessness and post twelve-hour shift fatigue looked eerily similar. He placed his tray on the metal rails of the counter and slowly pushed it along as the line moved forward. Only one other staff member was using the rail while everyone else held their trays in their hands. He wondered why everyone didn't use the convenience of the rail, then wondered why he even cared. The line progressed along, and Josh could now overhear the short exchanges between cafeteria-goers and Sally. She was pleasant enough, but years of repetitive motions, both physical and mental, had left her on autopilot.

"Mornin', Sally," Josh said as he slid his tray to the edge of the railing.

Sally acknowledged him while at the same time punching in prices of items she had long ago memorized and then memorized again and again as the ever-increasing price of inflation brought the cost of food and practically everything else up over her many years of employment.

"Five seventy-five," Sally noted, finally looking up at Josh.

"Oh, shoot, I forgot. Can you add a bagel, two cream cheeses, and an iced caramel cappuccino?" He had almost forgotten to grab Kim her post-shift snack. After adding the items, Josh handed Sally his hospital ID. It served as his time card, access pass, and would even deduct any food expenditures from his upcoming paycheck. The prices in the cafeteria weren't the best, but unlike the stereotypical quality of hospital food perpetuated in

## The Virtue of Vices – Jeremy McShurley

pop culture references, Princemoore Memorial had some of the best food in town. There were some who even joked that they had injured themselves just to get a good meal, though the cafeteria was technically open to the public as well.

Josh walked over to the condiment table and set his tray down. He placed his plate into a togo container then put it into a bag with some napkins, a plastic spork, and knife. He then walked over to the pastries and grabbed a blueberry bagel and two onion and chive cream cheese spreads, a combination of flavors that Josh found inedible, but Kim found delectable. He then fixed her iced coffee, placed all three drinks into a carrier, and started making his way towards the elevators, just as the murmur and buzz of cafeteria activity started to grow. Throwing a couple of nods, winks, and hellos to his co-workers as he left, he smiled to himself as a feeling of comfort and familiarity washed over his body.

Humans are creatures of habit, a holdover of the instinctual survival mechanisms that had allowed the species to wander far from the hostile environment of Africa and spread to every corner of the Earth. But humans are also a creative animal. The combination of habit and ingenuity had given them mastery over the animal kingdom and a supposed dominion over all the other beasts of the world. Josh witnessed this strange dichotomy almost every day as a paramedic. The last several years had seen a dramatic uptick in drug-related incidences, mostly of the meth and heroin variety. And the economic depression that plagued the city's west side had led to frequent calls for either domestic abuse or child endangerment.

White River City was by no means a metropolis, but it was one of most populous cities in the state, home to both Princemoore University and his current employer, Princemoore Memorial Hospital. These were two of the city's largest employers, and Josh was relieved to have a job. He had moved here from his small rural town to attend PU as a freshman. But like many young men and women of his age, he found the transition to be more difficult than he believed it would be. By his second semester, he was on academic probation, due mostly to a lack of scholastic focus and a distracting social life.

Josh had been generally insulated from national politics in his hometown, but upon entering the vibrant and expressive culture of the marketplace of ideas, he was easily drawn into the presidential campaign of then Senator Barack Obama. He had only been eleven years old when the Twin Towers fell, and the conservative nature of his family and fellow townsfolk tried to imbue him with fervent, patriotic-fueled support for the War on Terror. But even as a child he abhorred the idea of war. Pictures and films on the subject caused him so much distress that he swore off history channels long ago. So when his roommate dragged him to an off-campus event one evening, it was no surprise Josh found himself bonded to the anti-war rhetoric of Students for Perpetual Peace.

Josh found his suspension from school to be a blessing in disguise. It gave him the time to travel with the SPP as they moved from city to city protesting the activities of their government. He never moved into a leadership role with the group, finding that others had the verbal savvy he had never developed, nor really desired to develop. He was far better at studying the topics his group supported, and he provided countless hours of research to the planning and speech-writing committees. By the 2012 election, though, he like many others had become disillusioned with President Obama, noting that the Hope and Change he had promised was nothing more than a slogan. The wars continued, and Josh's efforts at ending the bloodshed seemed to be all for naught. So, after Obama's reelection, Josh returned to Princemoore University to earn his associate degree as a paramedic.

There was a more immediate feeling of satisfaction in his new field. While he had believed if enough people protested the War on Terror it would come to an end, the results of the SPP's activities only garnered occasional accolades. War had simply become a way of life, albeit a different life than The Greatest Generation. His grandparents had fought against the evils of Fascism, his parents Communism, while his generation was in a never-ending war against radical Islam, Muslim extremism, global terror, or whatever other term was the talking point of the day. Although his grandparents and their fellow countrymen had sacrificed everything to defeat Hitler and the Nazi war machine, his generation had only sacrificed their lives, limbs, and perhaps, their innocence.

So instead of turning a weapon on strangers in some far off town, Josh turned his medical training to the strangers of his new home, White River City. Josh did his best to follow in the teachings of all the great peacemakers of the world, especially Mahatma Gandhi who said, "You must be the change you wish to see in the world." Failing at ending war, he instead sought to treat the sick and wounded. His goal was to one day become a doctor, but he wanted to gain experience in the medical field as soon as possible. He planned on returning to school next year for his nursing degree, then eventually going on to medical school. His girlfriend, Kim, served as an inspiration, and he was excited to see her, even if it was only for a little bit. Their shifts weren't always in synch, as is the case for many in their professions, so he relished each precious moment.

Josh could hear what sounded like the end of a heated discussion coming from inside Kim's office. "I don't know what else to tell you, Kim. He doesn't want the treatment. Psych's already done an eval and found him competent…"

"But can't you…" interrupted Kim.

"I've pulled every string. I'm sorry, there's nothing else I can do. Just drop it…"

"But…"

"Drop it." The door suddenly swung open and, Dr. Graham made a hasty exit, nearly knocking the drink holder out of Josh's hand.

"Sorry," Dr. Graham quickly apologized, "Oh, hey, John, good to see you," and with that, the doctor was onto his next task.

Josh shook his head, thinking that even after working with Dr. Graham for several months, he still thought his name was 'John.' He entered Kim's office and set down the bag of food and the drink carrier. "Hi, hun. What was that all about?" he asked, giving her a peck on the cheek.

Kim sighed, "It's a long story."

"I've got half an hour 'til I'm on," Josh assured her, subtly encouraging her to continue.

Kim remained reluctant for a moment as she spread cream cheese on her bagel then took a drink of her iced coffee. She spun her office chair towards Josh and began.

The Virtue of Vices – Jeremy McShurley

Several staff members sprinted into room 307B after seeing every warning light go off at the nursing station, accompanied by a chorus of bells, beeps, and screeches. They quickly rushed to the aid of the only patient in the room, Reginald Holland. He was sitting up on the edge of the bed, his feet firmly planted on the floor. Reggie, as he was known to friends and relatives, was still in the process of taking out every tube and needle that had been stuck in him a couple of days ago.

"No, no, leave that in, Mr. Holland."

Reggie looked directly into the eyes of Kim Feinhorn then proceeded to yank his IV out of the vein in his left arm. "I don't want ya damn tubes and, I don't want ya damn medicine, woman," emphatically stated the elderly patient. Reggie spoke with a thick, black Southern accent, being originally from Alabama. His parents had been part of the Great Migration, where millions of African-Americans moved out of the Deep South to seek work in the factories of the North.

One of the nursing students started pressing buttons on Reggie's monitor, stopping the alarms. At that point, Reggie's attending physician, Dr. Graham, walked into the room.

"Looks like someone has a little pep in their step. Feeling better are we, Mr. Holland?" Dr. Graham casually walked over towards the bedside as most of the staff returned to the nurse's station.

Kim grabbed some antiseptic and tried to apply it to the IV's puncture point. Reggie pulled his arm back. "We don't want that to get infected," she explained and tried again.

"I don't see no point in fixin' up my arm when I'm gonna be dead in three months anyway," Reggie logically asserted.

"As I tried to explain, the treatment has a very high success rate, and if it works you may have another good ten years…" started Dr. Graham.

"I am 73 years old, Doc. I have had enough 'good ten years'," he interrupted. "You know the average life expectancy of a Black man in America?"

Dr. Graham did indeed know, but he feigned ignorance and Reggie continued.

"Seventy-two. Know what it is for a White man? Seventy-seven. I already done beat the odds. When it's your time, it's your time. I've seen shit over the years that'd turn your white-ass skin even whiter. So don't go tellin' me about no treatment. Black folks've had enough of your 'treatment'." Reggie had made his way over to the small closet next to the bathroom. He opened the door and started getting out his belongings.

Kim and Dr. Graham stood in silence, a bit taken aback by Reggie's tirade.

Reggie started to remove his hospital gown, "What? You gonna watch me change too?"

Dr. Graham pulled the privacy curtain and followed Kim out of the room and into the hallway.

"We can't let him leave," Kim pleaded.

"And we can't make him stay," Dr. Graham reminded her.

"Maybe I can talk to him, you know, talk some sense into him."

"It'll take an hour or so to finish up his discharge papers," Dr. Graham began calculating.

"What about a psych evaluation?" Kim suggested.

"He appears competent. He's not a danger to himself or anyone else."

"So, ripping an IV out of your arm isn't considered manic?" she argued.

Dr. Graham thought for a moment. "I believe Dr. Allen is still on. She owes me one. All right, you get his paperwork started and talk to him all you want, a lot of good it will do. And I'll see if Dr. Allen concurs with your 'mania' assessment. But no promises," he ended with the wag of his finger.

Kim knocked on the door to announce her presence. "Mr. Holland? We just have some paperwork for you to fill out, then you're free to go."

After a moment of silence she continued, "Are we decent?" Again there was nothing. Kim slowly pulled the privacy curtain aside, hoping Reggie was fully clothed. She saw him sitting at a small table underneath the room's only window, looking outside. He was wearing the same brown suit he had on when he was brought in Tuesday afternoon. She sat in the other chair and looked at him, wondering what he was staring at.

"It's ok to be scared, Mr. Holland," she began.

"I ain't scared. I already told ya, when it's your time…"

"…it's your time," she completed the statement, nodding and smiling. "What about your children, your grandchildren? Don't you want to see your grandchildren grow up?"

"Now, you just stop tryin' to guilt me right now, missy. They gonna have their own problems to deal with. No point in bringin' them into this," he argued.

"So, you aren't even going to tell them?"

"No, ma'am," he shook his head and pursed his lips.

Kim could tell from the look in Reggie's eyes that she was already starting to make some inroads. She had learned to read people over the years, and she was almost certain he was close to breaking. She just needed to find that one facet of his life that was worth living for.

"Alright, we just need you to fill out a few forms, Mr... Holland?" A nursing student from Princemoore University entered the room and walked towards the table.

"About time," Reggie exclaimed, turning his attention away from both the window and Kim.

Kim screamed in her head as the student went over each form, showing Reggie which i's to dot and t's to cross. As the two were going over his discharge procedure she poked her head into the hallway to see if Dr. Allen was anywhere in sight. Kim heaved a sigh of relief and she saw the resident psychiatrist casually walking around the corner from the nurse's station. She waved to get her attention.

"Over here, Dr. Allen."

Dr. Allen's gait sped up a bit and the two met just outside the room. "I understand the patient removed their IV on their own accord," she asked, making sure she had her story correct.

"Yes, doctor," Kim agreed. "He's refused treatment and is filling out his discharge forms right now. I've been trying to convince him to stay, but he's pretty bullheaded. Would you mind talking to him for a moment, maybe find some loophole?"

"He won't be the first patient to take out their IV. It's a pretty steep hill, to be honest. But Dr. Graham explained how much this meant to you. I'll have a chat with him."

"Thank you, thank you, thank you," Kim said with relief.

She heard Dr. Allen introduce herself and begin the evaluation. Kim was tempted to stay but felt it might overwhelm Mr. Holland, and instead returned to the nurse's station. She simply hoped that the shrink could springboard off of any progress she might have made with Mr. Holland.

Josh set his plate of food down on the desk, having eaten almost all of it during Kim's story. He leaned in and wrapped his arms around her, pulling her in tight. "You did your best, and that's all you can ask. In fact, you did more than your best. You've been doing this what, almost ten years? And you're still not jaded? That's an accomplishment in itself."

Kim leaned into Josh's chest, listening to his breathing and the sound of his beating heart. She felt herself finally start to relax, inhaling the smell of Josh's body wash and laundry detergent.

Josh released his embrace. "Well, I have to clock in here in a bit. And it looks like you still have some work to do."

"Yeah," Kim agreed. "Almost finished."

"You decided on the show tonight?" Josh asked with a few more bites of bacon and eggs in his mouth.

"I dunno. I'm pretty pooped. Plus, I have to work tomorrow, and this whole Mr. Holland thing's got me all drained. But, I would like to see them play. Did I tell you he went to my high school? He was a couple of years behind."

Josh chuckled, "Yeah, like, every time one of their songs comes on the radio."

Kim couldn't disagree with his statement. "I'll let you know later. I might just stop in for a bit. What time is it at?"

"Ten, ten-thirty." Josh looked at the clock on the wall. "I gotta get going," he kissed Kim on the cheek. "See you later, hun."

"Bye," Kim finally bit into her bagel and returned to her work.

Josh made his way to the garage and swiped his card with three minutes to spare. He began to go through his checklist, making sure the ambulance was clean and stocked. Once finished with that, he polished off the rest of his biscuits and gravy and tossed the container into the break room trashcan. One of the other paramedics came in sipping on an energy drink and munching on a granola bar.

"Hey, Josh."

"What's up, Jose?" The two sat down, although each had one ear trained to the dispatch radio. "So, I got a kinda weird question for you. What would you do if you only had a few months to live?'

Jose sat silently for a minute. "I'd go to Paris. I've always wanted to see Paris," he decided, daydreaming about the Eiffel Tower and fresh croissants.

"You wouldn't want to spend time with your family?" Josh asked, a little confused.

"Well, yeah, sure. I thought we were bein' all hypothetical," Jose responded, unsure of the seriousness of the question.

"Doesn't that feel a little selfish?" Josh inquired.

"You're the one who asked, and I'm just telling ya what I'd do. Might as well go out with a bang. I guess, when it's your time, it's your time."

The Virtue of Vices – Jeremy McShurley

**Promiscuity** - *(prom-i-skyoo-i-tee)*
Participating in sexual relations with multiple partners either casually or indiscriminately

Just south of the Princemoore University campus sat a neighborhood comprised mainly of student rentals along with a scattering of family homes and blighted properties. When its prominent namesake family first founded the university, the adjacent neighborhood was built to house the faculty and staff. The proximity provided a short commute for the university's employees as cars were a rarity at the time of its founding in the early 20th century. As the university grew in size and transportation allowed for faster travel times, the staff slowly began moving to other parts of the city, and the neighborhood began the transformation into its current incarnation. On the books the neighborhood was called University Heights. But the school's students referred to it by its better-known name, Drunken Acres.

Fridays and Saturdays were Drunken Acres' most active of nights, and this Friday was no different. School had been in session for just over a month or so and midterms were far from the minds of most of the students. Instead, former freshmen were now making their sophomore rounds, having returned to school with greater confidence and curiosity than the previous year. Although not specifically barred from Drunken Acres, there was an unspoken rule that freshmen were to indulge in their illicit activities either in the dorms or at the University Mall. For the most part, this rule was followed, but as with any unofficial social contract, exceptions were occasionally made.

In the years before cells and smartphones gained popularity, packs of raucous party-goers would walk, and later stumble, their way from house party to house party. As each group passed one another, they would exchange addresses of both where they had come from and where they were headed. It was a primitive form of analog social media, and it kept the parties raging until the sun came up, the kegs ran dry, or the cops finally came to shut down the houses that were dumb enough to draw attention. The packs of partiers still passed each other, but these days their eyes remained glued to their screens, either updating their profiles or following GPS directions to the next destination.

Nick Stone was in one of these groups of digital natives, accompanied by a couple of fellow seniors and a junior. Nick had two semesters left at P.U., and then it would be on to the search for a job and the true beginning of adulthood. At least, that's how the Brochure of Life had been presented to him as he grew up. In reality, becoming an adult was much further down the line than a degree and a 401k would lead one to believe. A century ago, being in your 20s meant you were almost halfway through your life. Today, the average American would live to be nearly 80, and that number will only increase as technology and medicine continue to advance. Twenty-first century citizens in their 20's weren't about to become adults; they were still figuring out how to be children.

"We almost there, Nick?" asked Alex, the junior. Alex had just turned 21 over the summer, and this would be his first semester as a legal drinker. Previous years had him scattering out the back doors of parties with all the other underage drinkers as the flashing blue and red lights of the campus police indicated it was time to go home. This year, he would be able to proudly hand his ID to the officer and say, "Here you are, sir."

"Huh? Uh, yeah, just a couple of blocks," Nick absent-mindedly replied.

"You ever been there before?"

"Yeah, it's cool. I know a couple of the guys from class. It's pretty laid back. I figure it's a good place to start the festivities." Alex looked at the time on his phone. It was just around eight.

Derrek pulled a glass piece filled with pot out of his pocket and took a toke. He coughed a bit, and then passed it to Chuck who continued the circle.

"'Ere," said Rod, holding in the smoke as long as possible and offering the bowl to Nick.

"Oh, no thanks, man."

The group stopped walking and stared at Nick, bewildered. In the time they had known him he had never passed up marijuana.

"What?" he asked, as though they had just accused him of being a werewolf. He smiled, realizing the group's confusion. "I got a drug test coming up for this internship…"

"Pussy."

"Faggot."

"I got a drug test coming up for this internship," mocked Rod with a high-pitched voice and dramatic gestures.

"Fuck off," Nick laughed, pushing Rod on the shoulder.

"Naw, it's cool, dude," Chuck conceded and began the group moving forward again.

Rod and Derrek went back to showing each other fail videos, cackling at the wounds being inflicted on social media buffoons.

"Did you tell Deena where this place is at?" asked Alex.

Chuck nodded, "Yup. Said she'd be there later."

"Dude, you better hit that shit this time. She's gonna think your junk don't work."

"In time, my friend, in time," Chuck responded, raising his shoulders and slowly tapping the tips of his fingers together.

"What are you waiting for? She's slept with, like, half the basketball team and a few of the football players. Now, I know you only play rugby, but... the girl likes jocks... and the girl likes cocks," Alex said, ending the joke in song.

"Ok, one, that's a bunch of locker room bullshit, and two, I really like this chick. I know I've poked my share of holes, but this girl's a keeper. I'm gonna be graduating next spring and I don't wanna spend the rest of my life chasin' tail. You, on the other hand, still have another couple years to play the field. But don't worry. Someday the Supreme Court will recognize same-sex marriages," Chuck laughed, patting Alex on the back.

"Dick," muttered Alex as he stopped berating his buddy.

The group climbed the steps of the front porch where they had just arrived at. Music could faintly be heard coming from inside, yet not loud enough to carry into the street and attract the attention of the authorities. A bearded fellow wearing a Princemoore University sweatshirt greeted them from a battered recliner.

"Fi' dolla," he prompted, holding up his fingers. Each of the guys paid the cover charge and made their way inside. After a quick glance around the room for familiar faces, the group parted ways and joined the crowded party.

## The Virtue of Vices – Jeremy McShurley

While most of the people meandering about Drunken Acres were looking for a good time, Justin Harlowe was looking for souls to save. His church taught that drinking and partying were nothing more than the evil influence of Satan. Every Friday and Saturday, Justin would walk around Drunken Acres, attempting to bring more members into his pastor's Flock. Most of the time he would approach the various groups of students as they made their way from party to party. On occasion, he would go into one of the parties, feeling there would be a larger crowd of potential converts. Justin had spotted Nick's group just a few moments ago, and he followed them to the house.

"Fi dolla," the bearded doorman requested.

"Oh, I'm not drinking," Justin replied and grabbed the doorknob.

"I don't care if you're not breathing. You want inside, you gotta pony up," the doorman stood up and gently nudged Justin away from the door with his chest.

"Fine," he pulled out his wallet and retrieved five singles, giving them to the doorman who then returned to his recliner.

Justin walked inside, immediately becoming overwhelmed by the smell of booze, cigarettes and pheromones. "The Lord is my light and my salvation... whom shall I fear? The Lord is the stronghold of my life... of whom shall I be afraid?" He walked over to a group of three students sitting on a couch up against the wall.

"Can I talk with you about our Savior, Lord Jesus?"

"Nick."

"Brittany." She extended her hand and accepted Nick's gentle handshake. Brittany was taller than average, 5'10 according to the listing on the volleyball players' roster. She was actually closer to 5'9, but sports teams tended to exaggerate the stats of their players in an attempt to intimidate opposing teams. She had recently cropped her light brown hair rather short, finally tiring of waiting for it to dry after hitting the showers. Her dark green eyes stared back into Nick's as she released her grip.

"I've seen you before," Nick noted.

Brittany raised one knee into the air and stood on the tiptoes of her other foot. She then raised her arm, slowly bringing it halfway down to her waist and grimaced, holding her position.

"Brittany Stoffer," Nick realized, wagging both index fingers towards her. "You made that game winning kill the other week against Harrold State." Nick remembered seeing Brittany on the cover page of P.U.'s newspaper, *The Daily Times.*

"The one and only," she smiled and shrugged, although feeling a bit uncomfortable at the sudden admiration.

Nick reached into a plastic tub of ice water and beer and pulled out two cans of cheap domestics. He began to offer one to Brittany but quickly pulled it back.

"Can I see some ID?" he asked, imitating the stern voice of a police officer.

Brittany slowly leaned forward, slightly exposing her cleavage under her peach blouse and shimmied her shoulders. In a breathy voice she responded, "How's this for my ID, officer?"

Nick chuckled and handed her the beer. "You're funny."

Brittany giggled, "You're cute."

## The Virtue of Vices – Jeremy McShurley

Some shouts from across the kitchen interrupted their flirting. They turned to face the ongoing game of beer pong where a small group of partiers had gathered. Two beefy guys were in the midst of high-fiving and backslapping, indicating their victory. The other team stepped away from the table and two more opponents took their place.

Nick and Brittany started back into their conversation when they noticed several red plastic cups filled with half finished beverages and cigarette butts began slightly bouncing on the kitchen counter they were standing next to.

"What the hell?" Nick wondered. The counter was abutted against a wall that led into a hallway. Nick went around the corner and started walking down the hall with Brittany following right behind. After a few feet they came to a door that led into the bathroom. They could hear a stream of thuds coming from inside that matched the rhythm of the cups in the kitchen. Nick placed his ear against the wall and Brittany quickly followed suit. The thuds became louder and were now accompanied by the grunts and moans of what could only be assumed to be an aggressive act of coitus.

Brittany silently mouthed the word "wow", while Nick made a circle with one hand and proceeded to insert and withdraw the index finger of his other.

Brittany's mouth dropped open in an embarrassed smile and she lightly smacked Nick on the arm. The aural voyeurs, now too invested in their snooping to stop, remained glued to the wall. The thudding, thumping, panting and groaning gradually increased in both volume and speed until they suddenly became nothing more than the sounds of heavy breathing.

The two pulled away from the wall and stood in silence for a moment, of which Nick then broke, "I think I need a cigarette after that."

"Ah do believe Ah have mahself a case of the vapors," Brittany said in a southern belle accent as she pantomimed waving a fan on her face.

Nick chuckled. "But seriously, I think I'm going outside for a smoke."

"You can smoke in here."

"Yeah, but it's that second hand smoke that'll kill ya," he joked and headed back into the kitchen then out through the side door with Brittany coming along.

Nick turned away from the wind and lit his cigarette, then turned back to face Brittany. "So, to pull a line from the *Freshman Handbook*, 'What are you studying?'"

"General Studies." She switched back into her fake accent, "But really Ah'm just lookin' for a man Ah can cook and clean for the rest of mah life."

Nick laughed and shook his head.

Brittany returned to her normal voice. "What about you?"

"Poli-sci."

"You going into government or law?"

"Actually, the opposite. I want to take the whole system down. 'If you know the enemy and know yourself, you need not fear the result of a hundred battles. If you know yourself but not the enemy, for every victory gained you will also suffer a defeat. If you know neither the enemy nor yourself, you will succumb in every battle'. Sun Tzu."

"You memorized that, huh?"

"Yeah, and a few other lines here and there. I just think that the whole thing is rigged. Democrat, Republican, it doesn't matter. They all work for the same corporations and billionaires that contribute to their campaigns. Just a bunch of… wait, sorry. I tend to ramble on about this stuff and end up losing people."

Brittany was amazed at Nick's passion. "No, I love it. Most of my friends just want to talk about who won the last *American Celebrity* or sports stuff. I admit I don't know a lot about politics, but I should. It's just so confusing."

Nick stomped out his cigarette into the ground. "That's what they want you to think. They want you smart enough to pull the lever, but not smart enough to ask what the lever does. But it's like anything, the more you read up on it, the clearer it becomes."

"You are an interesting fella, Nick."

"And you are a kind and patient gal, Brittany Stoffer."

From there the world around Nick and Brittany stopped spinning, and the two became lost in a moment of their own creation. Conversations don't always come easily to strangers, as the person you are and the person you want to portray come into constant conflict. That initial presentation of self, more generally known as first impressions, is tough to recover from when it is either misrepresented or misinterpreted. But other times the stars and planets align, and the words that are exchanged between two people come with such ease and natural cadence, that they appear to have been written by the goddess Venus herself.

Nick had burned through multiple cigarettes, as he tended to do when he got on a roll. But he could tell that Brittany was genuinely absorbing everything he was throwing at her, and her questions were sincere and in the interest of gaining knowledge.

"Wow. Wow," she slightly shook her head back and forth. "So this small group of people run the world?"

"That's sort of the *Cliff's Notes* version. When it comes down to it, it's the system itself and not so much the people running the system. But until you get rid of the existing system, there can't be a replacement. So, we got to take it down. Like a forest fire burns all the old dead trees away, so new saplings can grow from the ashes."

"Sun Tzu?"

"Oh, no, that's mine." Throughout the whole conversation, Nick and Brittany had been slowly moving closer towards one another, unconscious of their motion. Nick suddenly wished he hadn't been smoking so many cigarettes as he began to lean forward to gently brush his lips against hers.

"Get outta here, ya Jesus freak!"

Nick's attempt was suddenly interrupted by the loud bang of the side door being slammed open and what appeared to be an adult male being pushed down the stone steps that led to the kitchen.

"Whoa, whoa, whoa. What's going on?" Nick asked as he put himself between the fallen male and his attacker.

Brittany quickly rushed to the aid of the 'Jesus freak'. "Are you alright?" she questioned, trying to help him up.

"I'm, ok, thanks," replied Justin with a tinge of pain in his voice.

By now a few other people were making their way outside to investigate the ruckus. Nick had managed to calm down Justin's attacker and had pulled him back inside. One of the party's hosts came out to check on the situation.

## The Virtue of Vices – Jeremy McShurley

"Hey, everyone needs to calm down. You want the cops coming?" asked the host. He walked over to Justin who was now standing by himself. "You ok?"

"Lord Jesus will heal my wounds, today, and for Eternity." Justin rubbed his hands together to remove the bits of gravel that had been embedded in them.

"That's… good to know." By now everyone had gone back inside and the host stood alone with Justin. "Here," the host handed Justin a five. "Look, you seem like a nice guy, but you're weirding everyone out. People are here to have a good time, not get saved. But, good luck," the host concluded with a look of pity on his face.

Justin handed back the five to the host as he was walking away. "You can use this for someone who doesn't have enough." He then disappeared into the shadows of Drunken Acres.

Nick walked back outside to continue his conversation with Brittany. He and some of the house roommates had spent the last few minutes trying to calm down Justin's attacker. The guy was drunk and it was finally suggested that he go home and sleep it off, which he agreed to do.

"Brittany? You still out here?" Nick questioned into the night air. Receiving no answer he climbed the short steps back into the kitchen and scanned the room. Nick proceeded to move from room to room, calling her name.

Alex saw Nick from across the living room and wormed his way through the mass of dancing and chatting people.

"There you are. Where've you been?" Alex asked.

"I met this really awesome chick. She has short brown hair, green eyes, she's wearing a sorta light pink shirt." Nick continued looking around. He went back into the kitchen with Alex following.

"Hmm," Alex thought. " I think I remember seeing her earlier but not for awhile."

"Yeah, we were talking outside for awhile and now she's just gone."

"Did you get her number?" Alex asked, thinking of the obvious.

"Crap. No, I didn't get that far. She just sorta vanished." The collection of beverages on the kitchen cabinet suddenly began bouncing again. Nick smiled at Alex. "Dude, you gotta come check this out."

The Virtue of Vices – Jeremy McShurley

**Rage** - *(reyj)*
Emotional expression that manifests in bouts of uncontrollable anger or hatred

There were two strip clubs in White River City. One, The Queen of Hearts, was on the west side of town near the old manufacturing district. During its heyday, the city's factory workers would take their hard-earned money and tuck wrinkled singles into the g-strings of countless erotic dancers. At the time it was the only gentlemen's club in town and quite a few Princemoore University students worked the pole when they weren't working on their studies. In those days, a few hours of dancing a week could pay for rent, groceries, and even tuition. Today the place was lucky to keep the lights on, and most of its patrons were spending their unemployment checks instead of their monthly bonuses.

A second club opened on the north side in the early 1980's to accommodate the growing population in Santa Mesa. While Santa Mesa didn't allow the club to be built within town limits, the owners found a location just across the border. That gave suburban husbands the chance sneak off in the middle of the night and still return home safely before their wives even knew they were gone. Today, Caligula's Parlor was the gentlemen's club of choice for both the well to do of Santa Mesa and the makers and shakers of White River City.

Peter Princemoore pulled into Caligula's parking lot with the windows down and the heavy metal blaring. The lot was full, as usual for a Friday night. So he made his own space by pulling his black G70 Illuminato up onto the sidewalk, scratching the bottom frame of the low riding sports car. Peter had just made the short drive from Deerwood Hills

Country Club where the bar's last call had forced the remaining members and their guests to take leave for the evening.

The doorman cast a quick glance towards the vehicle then turned away. Peter cranked up the volume on the stereo and opened the center console, pulling out a small baggie of white powder, a mirror, and a short straw. He dumped some of the cocaine onto the mirror and used a business card to form it into two thick lines. Peter bent forward and snorted the coke into each of his nostrils, deeply sniffing several times. After that, he gathered the remaining powder onto his index finger, rubbed it onto his gums and licked his teeth. He then put the mirror and straw back into the console, slipped the baggie into his sport coat's inner pocket and turned off the vehicle.

Peter walked over to the doorman, a hulking male who looked as though he was about to burst out of his black business suit. "Hey, chief. You mind moving that when another spot opens up?" Peter asked pointing towards his car. Before the doorman could answer, he put the keys and a hundred dollar bill into his hand. "Thanks, chief," said Peter again sniffing a few times. The doorman put the keys and money into his pocket and returned to his duties.

Peter then went around to the rear of the building where the loading dock was located. He tugged at the gate, but it was latched from the inside. Peter pulled out his wallet and retrieved one of his credit cards. He slipped the card into a slit in the fence and pushed the latch mechanism up, opening the door. Peter stepped into the loading dock and walked towards the back door that he discovered to be unlocked. He entered the building and found himself in the kitchen area where the banging and clanging of pots and pans permeated the air. As he headed out of the kitchen, he walked by the heat lamps and grabbed a handful of French fries off of a random plate.

Caligula's Parlor was full, perhaps even over capacity. There were three girls on the square shaped main stage in the center of the room. In the corners were smaller round stages with a pole in the middle and a dancer was on each one of those as well. To Peter's left ran a huge bar along the entire wall. On the other side was a mirrored wall with a low platform that ran along the entire length. Ten poles were set staggered into the platform, although only a couple were occupied at the time. He couldn't see them from here, but Peter knew that towards the front entrance were doors that led into the private dancing rooms.

The swinging kitchen doors suddenly opened, and a server came busting out with a tray in hand. The edge of the tray smacked into Peter's back, and the server dropped several plates of food onto the floor while spilling some of it on Peter's jacket. He grunted and turned around.

"What the fuck, you fucking retard!" he screamed at the server.

"Oh my God, oh shit. I'm so sorry. I didn't see you there," she responded apologetically. The waitresses at Caligula's were just as attractive as the dancers, although they wore skimpy black dresses instead of going topless. The server, a tiny brunette with pigtails, set the tray on the ground and started putting the plates onto it.

"So you're blind and retarded? Great, nice hiring job," Peter noted as he removed his sports coat. He looked at the back of it. "Oh, and you got ranch and wing sauce all over it. Jesus."

By now a manager had made his way over. "Mr. Princemoore, I am very sorry. Is there anything I can do?"

The server had managed to pick up the mess and was standing back up with the tray of scattered food.

"Yeah, you can fire this dumb bitch," he said, pointing to the server, whose eyes immediately filled with tears.

"Please, no. I need this job. It won't happen again," she pleaded.

The manager shook his head. "I'm sorry, Vickie. Mr. Princemoore is a very special guest. We're going to have to let you go. You can pick up your last check next Tuesday."

Vickie's tears turned into heaving sobs as she dropped the tray, covered her eyes, and ran crying into the kitchen area.

"Aww, now she got shit all over my shoes," Peter said looking down. "And what about this?" he asked pointing at the mess on his jacket.

"Again, my apologies, sir. Just send us the bill for the dry cleaning." The manager's face was flush with embarrassment.

Peter took a deep breath. "That's why they put you in charge, Mason. I assume my table is available."

"Yes, of course, Mr. Princemoore. Are we expecting any guests tonight?" Mason asked. He grabbed another server as she started walking into the kitchen. "Clean this up," he ordered, pointing at the mess on the floor.

"No, I'm flying solo tonight. But you could send over a bottle of MacClambroch 18. And send me over one of the girls. You know my type." Peter began heading towards his spot at the back of the room.

"Yes, of course, Mr. Princemoore. Right away," Mason responded and hastily followed Peter's orders.

Peter sat down at his table, although technically it was reserved for anyone in his family. But Peter was the only member to frequent the establishment, so in essence, it was his. He used the tablecloth to wipe the sauce from his shoes and sport coat that he then folded and set down beside him. The table was large and round and the cushioned seating curved around it leaving a few feet at the front to get into the space. The server who had cleaned up the mess from earlier hustled to him and set down a bottle of scotch, two glasses, and a small bucket with ice and a pair of tongs.

"Kameron will be over in just a moment," she said.

"Good." Peter handed the girl a folded twenty.

By now Peter's cocaine had really started to kick in. He bobbed his head to the beat of the techno music, of which all the girls were dancing to. He found himself staring at the intricate light show that was accompanying the performances of the dancers on the center stage. After a couple of minutes, he caught movement out of the corner of his eye.

"Hi, Peter. Mason wanted me to come join you this evening. I'm Kameron." Unlike the rest of the girls, Kameron was wearing a thin white t-shirt that exposed her midriff. Her thong panties were also white with sparkling faux jewelry running along the top. Kameron had a full set of lips, a tiny button nose, and long luscious lashes. Her blonde hair was shoulder length mingled with streaks of pink and blue.

Peter scooted to his right to give her plenty of room to sit down, which she did. He dropped a couple of ice cubes into each glass and poured a heavy amount of scotch into both glasses. "Cheers," he offered, and Kameron tapped her glass to his.

"Cheers," she responded then took a small sip of the drink and set it down.

Peter, on the other hand, slammed the entire glass, set it down and filled it again. "Down the hatch," he said, nodding towards her beverage.

Kameron giggled and let her hair flip about her face. "I'm such a lightweight," she explained.

Peter grabbed her glass from off the table, drank the whole thing, slid his newly poured one towards her and said, "Not tonight."

Kameron put the glass to her lips and tilted it back. Though aged eighteen years, the scotch still burned her throat on the way down. She willed herself from coughing then slammed the glass onto the table. "Woo!"

Peter slid closer to Kameron and put his hand on her thigh as he filled their glasses again, adding a little more ice. "How about a private dance?"

"Not for another hour or so. Rooms are booked," she let him know, sipping on her drink whenever Peter did.

"Then I guess we'll just have to get another room," Peter suggested.

"I'm not really supposed to leave 'til end of my shift," Kameron explained as Peter continued to caress her thigh.

Peter reached into his sport coat and pulled out a golden money clip filled with cash. Kameron noticed an etching on the clip; a cross on a shield with a puma's claws clutching the side and its head atop the shield. She immediately recognized it as the Princemoore family crest. Peter pulled money from the clip and started slowly flipping hundred dollar bills onto the table, one after the other. "You go ahead and tell me when your shift is over."

Kameron couldn't believe her luck as Peter drove them through the countryside at speeds of more than 80 miles per hour. Just a few hours earlier she had been offered a new job, and the stack of hundreds that Peter had given her was going to be great relocation cash. It wasn't that she hated working at Caligula's; in fact, she loved it. Unlike many of her fellow dancers, who spent a good portion of their earnings on drugs and booze, Kameron lived within her means. She knew she wasn't going to be a dancer forever, but the recent opportunity was too good to pass up. Normally she would have never gone home with a stranger from the club, but this was a Princemoore, White River City's distinguished family. Peter hadn't told her where they were going, but she felt relatively safe with him, as long as he didn't wrap the car around a telephone pole.

"You want some blow?" Peter asked, yelling over the sounds of growling metal music.

"I'm ok, thanks," Kameron yelled back. "How much longer?"

"Not long. We're taking the back way," he explained. As the stars dimmed and the lights of the city brightened, Peter slowed down his speed, eventually turning onto Princemoore Avenue. He then began maneuvering through the curvy brick road neighborhood of the East Bank District.

Kameron looked in wonderment at the various mansions that comprised this part of town. When she was a kid, she used to ride her bike here with her friends and dream of living in one of these luxurious homes. But that was years ago, and those fantasies were far behind her.

Peter stopped the car just outside of a large, wrought iron gate with the word "Tymborlyn" shaped out of the metal at the very top. He reached out of the window and entered a passcode on the keypad causing the gate to open.

The last time Kameron had been to Tymborlyn was ten years ago when she came on a middle school field trip to visit the orchard. She didn't remember much about that trip, except for that Thadeus Princemoore had built Tymborlyn not long after the end of the Civil War. Much of the estate was open to the public, but Peter drove towards Tymborlyn Manor instead. As they approached the mansion Peter turned and drove around the giant fountain that stood out front. He then took a small driveway to the side of the manor and parked the car under one of the many giant oak trees.

Kameron got out and started looking around at her surroundings while Peter stayed in the car and did more cocaine. She felt as though she was in a fairy kingdom. All around her were huge trees and stone statues of mythological gods and creatures. Up ahead was a short path that led to a garden with a gazebo in the center. She started to walk that way when she heard what sounded like what might be a small fountain. She turned around to see Peter urinating on a statue of Pan. Kameron averted her eyes until he had finished, pretending not to notice.

"Come on, I'll give you the tour," Peter instructed while sniffing and rubbing his nose.

The Virtue of Vices - Jeremy McShurley

Kameron had hoped he was going to walk her around the grounds, but instead, he took her back around to the front entrance. Again he punched in a code, and the door unlocked. The main foyer was enormous, illuminated by a giant crystal chandelier. The floor was made of marble squares, alternating between black and white. Two suits of armor stood just to the left and right of the doorway and a large red rug embroidered with the family crest rested in the center of the room. About fifty feet ahead were several doorways leading to other parts of the mansion. Along the walls to the left and right were wide curving staircases leading up to the balcony above.

"The bedrooms are upstairs," Peter told Kameron as he began to climb the right staircase.

"How about that tour?" she requested.

"How about that fucking lap dance I paid good money for," he retorted from halfway up the stairs.

It was hard for Kameron to argue, as Peter had given her $1300 to come with him. While a few of the dancers were known to partake in "extracurricular dances," as they were known, Kameron had never done so. She made enough money the old fashioned way, and she wasn't about to start now. For the amount of money Peter had laid down, she figured he might be assuming they would be having sex tonight. But she had already planned everything out. Once he started coming down from the coke he would begin feeling the effects of the booze. She'd keep him talking for a while, teasing him from afar. Eventually, she'd start her lap dance. Once he finished she guessed he would lay back and fall asleep, giving her a chance to call a cab and head home, never to see him again.

"Yeah, sorry. I'm just a little blown away by this place," she said as she began ascending the stairs.

Peter let her catch up, "I'll give you something to blow."

Kameron smiled and laughed, "You are so funny," then dropped her expression the minute Peter turned around.

The two reached the top of the stairs, about twenty feet off the first floor. "Are we the only ones here?" Kameron asked.

"We better be. No one's lived here for years. The historical something or other takes care of the place. I just come here to party sometimes," Peter said as he opened one of the bedroom doors just off the balcony. "Welcome to 'Peter's Parlor.' Get it, like Caligula's Parlor?"

"Oh, you and your jokes," Kameron fake laughed again.

Peter turned on the lights and walked in with Kameron right behind.

"This is bigger than my whole apartment," she said in amazement.

Peter strutted over to the bed, a large king size with posts to the ceiling and curtains around the top. He sat on the edge and took off his shoes. "I'm waiting," he said impatiently.

"Any music?" she asked, trying to stall.

"Man, Mason, might have nailed you on the looks, but you are one pushy broad. Fine," Peter pulled his phone from his sport coat and started his playlist.

"That's a little heavy. Let's start this out nice and slow," Kameron requested, again trying to take up time.

Peter shook his head and picked a slower tempo song. "Is that ok?"

## The Virtue of Vices – Jeremy McShurley

"That's more than ok. That's perfect." Kameron removed her jacket and tossed it onto a nearby desk, showing off the outfit she was wearing when she initially met Peter. She gyrated and swerved to the beat, leisurely moving towards the bed. She stood in front of Peter and pulled her t-shirt up over her head then danced towards one of the bedposts. Treating it like a stripper pole, she wrapped her leg around it and started climbing upward, hoping it was as sturdy as it looked.

At that point Peter, undid his pants and began playing with himself. Kameron was a little worried at first but then decided that he might finish himself off and make her job all that much easier. She noticed he kept going faster and faster, grunting all the while and scrunching his face. Kameron moved from post to post, making certain to stay just out of Peter's reach. She noticed that he was having trouble becoming fully aroused.

"Come on. Dance better. Do it better," he kept saying over and over, getting louder each time.

Kameron had moved back towards the middle of the room. She crossed her arms over her breasts. "What's a matter? Little Petey doesn't wanna play?" she asked in a baby voice.

Before she could react, Peter had jumped off the bed and had grabbed her by the shoulders, "It's you!" he screamed. "You can't dance. This is your fault."

Kameron was terrified. Peter's pupils nearly filled his irises and spit flew from his mouth as he yelled. She jerked back and broke free from his grasp. Kameron looked over at her jacket on the desk. In its pockets were a small knife and some mace. She started to make a move towards it but Peter struck her across the face with a backhand causing her to see stars.

"This never happens. It's you! It's all your fault!"

Kameron turned to run towards the stairs. Peter was just behind and grabbed her by the shoulders again. He spun her around and shook her over and over, moving her backward. "Who the hell taught you to dance? You're the worst I've ever seen. This is all your fault!"

Peter pushed her away in frustration with his last verbal onslaught. Kameron stumbled back and lost her balance. Her waist arched up against the balcony railing and the momentum sent her slipping over the top. In a desperate attempt, Peter reached out his hand and grasped at the air. There was a short scream then a thud and a wet crunch. He looked over the edge but all Peter saw was red.

The Virtue of Vices – Jeremy McShurley

**Spite** - *(spahyt)*
Taking action for the purpose of annoying or causing emotional pain to someone else

*"We're still following the breaking news from earlier in the morning when apparently a gunman opened fire killing several people at a coffee shop in White River City. That was the Beanstalk Cafe, right, Gordy?"*
*"Yes, Leon. Beanstalk Cafe, located just off Princemoore University campus in the University Mall."*
*"Again, our hearts and prayers go out to all of those involved and their friends and family. This… this is just tragic… not the way we expected to spend the last hour of our marathon. I'm just… I'm just sickened. Gordy, you've been keeping up on the social media chatter. What's new on BlurtOut?"*
*"Here's a few more Blurts. '@wrcpd Beanstalk gunman still on loose. Perp considered armed and dangerous. Last seen wearing brown robes and wooden mask. #beanstalkshooting'. '@PrincemooreU Shelter in place warning still in effect for all of campus. Visit princemoore.edu for updates. #beanstalkshooting'. '@pumafan2016 still crazy at the Mall. Police everywhere. Trying to get closer for pics. Counted seven body bags so far #beanstalkshooting'. '@wrc-cityhall Mayor to make statement within hour. Contact officials if you have any information #beanstalkshooting'."*
*"Thank you for those updates, Gordy. We were planning on having Charlotte Wells this hour to talk about her new book,* Whale of a Tale: A Biography of Herman Melville. *Our apologies, Charlotte. We'll try to have you back next week. Instead, we are going to continue to follow the news*

*on the Beanstalk Cafe. Ok, hold on, I'm being told we have a witness from the shooting. Go ahead, caller."*

*"My name is Eli. I was there when everything went down."*

*"You were inside the coffee shop?"*

*"Yes. Yes, Leon. Me. Me and some buddies, we were playing cards in the Roth Room."*

*"Ok, now what is the Roth Room?"*

*"It's the part that used to be that old general store."*

*"Alright, yes. I'd never heard it called that before. Sorry, go on."*

*"Yeah, so, we were in the Roth Room when we heard the first shot. At first we thought it was maybe something from the counter, like, I dunno, like one of those big trays getting dropped. Then we heard it again and we knew... we knew it was gunshots. Sorry, I'm just, sorta seeing it all again."*

*"It's ok, Eli. Take your time."*

*"Yeah, ok. So, everyone, there were, like, maybe ten or twelve of us in there, so, everyone starts freaking out. Screaming. I kinda froze up, but my buddy grabbed my arm and started pulling me towards the exit. A bunch of us sorta got jammed up at the door, ya know, all pushing and stuff."*

*"Did you get a look at the shooter?"*

*"Not a real good look. Some old dude. I saw him get shot. It looked like maybe the shooter had on robes. I think it they were black, maybe brown. That's the last thing I saw before I got outside and started running."*

*"That's quite a story, Eli. Thank you for giving our listeners a little insight into tonight's tragedy. We're very glad you and your friends made it out safely."*

## The Virtue of Vices – Jeremy McShurley

> *"Thanks. Thank you, Leon. I feel really blessed, really blessed."*
> *"So, let me ask you…"*

The night audit of the Pay n' Stay Lodge turned the volume down on his radio, thinking he had heard the bell from the front desk. He got up from his office chair and went to check out the entryway. Again, he heard the bell ringing, and he noticed a male and female standing at the door. After giving a quick assessment, he decided they posed no threat and buzzed them in. But just to be safe, he grabbed a hold of the pistol that was strapped to the underside of the front desk.

"Good morning," he greeted them. "You haven't seen a guy wearing robes and a mask around here, have you?"

"Huh?" asked the male.

"Never mind," replied the night audit as the male and his companion approached the desk.

They both looked to be in their twenties or perhaps early thirties. The woman was beautiful, wearing a tight fitting red dress, matching high heels, and long silver earrings. The night audit guessed she was probably Mexican. The guy she was with had on jeans, a flannel shirt, and a jean jacket with different kinds of buttons pinned all over it. The two could not have been any more disparate in appearance.

Of course, the Pay n' Stay saw couples like these two on a nightly basis. The lodge had three types of rates; hourly, daily, and weekly, although anyone who paid for a month's lodging got a small discount. Decades ago, when the factories on the city's west side still pumped out their slew of goods, the Pay n' Stay was known as the Opossum Creek Lodge, named after the small waterway that used to run behind it. It was located just off of Highway 17 and at one time was a favorite for visiting businessmen. But as White River City's fortunes shrank, and then relocated to the east of the river, the number of visiting businessmen withered along with it. Even Opossum Creek disappeared in the early 90's as the spring that supplied the White River tributary finally dried up. The Pay n' Stay became a favorite stomping ground for lonely truckers, drug addicts, and one night secret rendezvous.

"We need a room please," the male looked at the night audit's nametag, "Chris."

"Yeah, we have a few available. How long will you be staying with us?" asked Chris as he pointed to a sign on the desk with the going rates.

The male looked over at the attractive female. "So, what, an hour?"

She gently slapped him on the chest. "Oh, you better last longer than an hour."

He smiled and turned back to Chris. "We'll take it for the day."

Chris began typing information into a computer terminal with a large, monochrome monitor and the kind of keyboard you could hear through the walls.

"Name please?" he prompted

"Bren...son. George Brenson" the male lied, changing his answer at the last second.

"And how will you be paying?"

George pulled out some money from his pocket. "Cash".

"That'll be $47.85 which includes towel fees and tax," Chris informed his new guests.

"Here you go." George handed Chris fifty dollars.

"And let me get your change," Chris began.

## The Virtue of Vices – Jeremy McShurley

"Oh no, that's alright," said the beautiful woman. She handed him a twenty-dollar bill. "For your troubles," she finished with a wink.

"No trouble at all, ma'am," Chris said as they concluded the transaction. He fully understood the purpose of the tip, as it wasn't the first time he had been subtly asked to forget he ever saw someone. Chris handed the couple their key and told them where their room was as well as the ice machine and vending area. "Enjoy your stay. Just dial star nine to ring the front desk." The two laughed as they left the office building, leaning into one another while they walked away. Chris went back into the office and turned the radio back up.

George chuckled to himself. In reality, his name was Brent Carmichael and the woman at his side was named Maria. He hadn't asked her what her last name was and there was a good chance he might never find out. Maria had been one of the last people on the dance floor at his place of employment, a music club called Holidaze. It had ended up being the busiest night Brent had even seen there as either a patron or employee. The headlining act was a band called Caleb Brown and the Skunk Munkies. They had gotten their start at Holidaze but managed to grow their fan base all across the country, even getting significant radio play. Maria was one of several hundred to come to the show, but she managed to catch Brent's attention from his vantage point up in the sound booth.

He had noticed her come into the venue pretty early in the night with a group of other ladies. As the night progressed and each one became more inebriated, their numbers slowly whittled down until only Maria was left. She and a few regulars were grooving to the tunes that Brent had been playing over the sound system since Caleb's band had ended their encore hours earlier. Not even the house lights coming up and the staff cleaning could peel her off the floor. Normally Brent would have shut the music down, but Maria's sultry look and gracious movements enamored him. Eventually one of the bouncers began to escort her towards the door.

"That's ok, Lucas. She's with me," Brent called out from the booth.

"Oh, sorry, Brent," Lucas said. "I didn't know." The bouncer walked away and began picking up plastic cups from the tables in the bar area.

Maria walked towards the sound booth from where Brent was coming down. "Thanks for inviting me tonight, Brent," she said, a little louder than necessary. She leaned in to give him a hug and whispered in his ear, "I'm Maria, by the way."

Brent gave her a peck on the cheek. "I'm glad you could make it, Maria. Did you want to dance some more?"

"Only if you'll dance with me," she insisted, pulling him onto the dance floor.

Brent was impressed with her apparent sobriety. He had watched her go to the bar on ten to twelve occasions throughout the evening, and that was just the times he noticed. But Brent had been sipping on drinks throughout the show as well, and it was difficult for him to detect the amount of booze that was on her breath. He assumed she must be drunk but at this point didn't really care. From the way Maria was rubbing up against him as they danced he was almost certain these moves were a prelude to another type of dance they were to partake in later on.

Upon catching a sideways glance from his manager, Brent knew it was time to move the party elsewhere. Maria was spinning around just a few feet from him, and he gently grabbed her by the shoulders to look into her dark eyes. "We gotta go. My boss just gave me the stink eye," he explained.

Maria spun towards a table where a middle-aged gentleman wearing a button up shirt was sitting with a small stack of papers and a laptop in front of him. "Hi!" she waved. "Thank you, I had a wonderful time tonight." She then grabbed Brent by the hand and started walking towards the door.

"Are we going back to your place? Or, did you want to come over to mine," he wondered, preferring his as it made him feel more comfortable in a home environment.

"I have a place in mind," Maria said before sprinting off towards her car.

The Pay n' Stay Lodge consisted of three buildings forming a U-shape plus the main office at the front of the complex. At one time there had been a picnic area down by where the Opossum Creek once ran. But the shelter had caught fire a few years ago and the new owners never spent the money to fix it. The days of picnics and summertime swimming were long gone. At both ends of each building was a set of stairs that led to the second-floor balcony. Brent and Maria held hands as they climbed the stairs of Building 3 on the way to their room.

It was still dark outside and the Sun was a couple of hours from breaking the horizon. Most of the part-time residents of the Pay n' Stay were asleep by now, even the junkies and prostitutes. They reached the door to their room, and Brent inserted the key. He held his breath for a second, unsure of the condition the room might be in. He let out a small sigh of relief as he flipped on the light switch just to the left of the door. The room was in considerably decent shape, considering the lodge's name and reputation. It was small, and the bed took up a majority of the space. There was a mirrored dresser just a few feet from the foot of the bed and two nightstands on each side. In the corner was a small table with a single chair sitting next to it. Towards the back of the room appeared to be a closet and a door that led into the bathroom.

"Wow, this place is about the same size as my apartment," Brent noted. "I think I know where I'm moving when my lease is up,"

Brent barely finished his sentence before Maria had grabbed him by the back of the head and shoved her tongue into his mouth. He quickly relaxed and eagerly returned the kiss, sliding his hands down along Maria's curvy hips. Maria pulled back with a smacking sound. "Ok, you passed the kiss test."

Brent reached up and gently cupped Maria's face with both hands. He could tell she was pretty back at the club, but this was really the first time he had a chance to truly become aware of her intricate features. He gently rubbed his thumb over a thin white scar on her left cheek.

"Where did this come from?" he asked her.

Maria slowly back away and kicked off her shoes, then reached down and pulled her dress up over her head, revealing nothing more than a lacy red bra and matching panties. She jumped towards the bed, bouncing up and down a few times before eventually settling on her side.

"A drug dealer from Nicaragua gave it to me. Come here," she commanded as she patted the other side of the bed.

Brent did as requested, removing his jacket and shirt on the way and tossing them onto the floor.

He lay down next to Maria who began to unbutton his pants as he started kissing her neck and shoulders.

"That's funny you noticed my scar. My husband never notices things like that anymore," she said as she pulled down Brent's zipper.

Brent choked and coughed into Maria's shoulder then pushed himself away. "Husband?"

"It's fine," she reassured him, and then started to nibble on his chest. "He's been sleeping around with someone else for awhile. Always coming home late, never wanting to make love. He brought this upon himself," she finished as she pulled off Brent's jeans and underwear and stood up at the foot of the bed.

"Wow," she exclaimed as she looked over Brent's naked body. "Do all you sound guys carry that much ammunition?" Maria got onto her knees and began kissing Brent's ankles. She then slowly started making her way up towards his crotch.

Brent closed his eyes and tried to allow himself to become fully aroused. But the thoughts of Maria's husband kicking in the door and killing them both made that difficult.

"So, um. Your husband. You caught him sleeping with someone else?" he asked, trying to figure a way to back out of this situation.

"I found enough evidence. If he's going to get some action on the side, then I might as well too. It's only fair, right? I suppose it was eventually going to happen. Ladies love a guy in uniform."

"Uniform? Your husband's in the army?"

"No," she said looking up from between Brent's legs. "He's a cop."

Brent pushed himself backward and sat up with his back against the headrest. "A cop?" he shouted in a voice more high-pitched than he had anticipated. "A cop?" he asked again, this time in a lower tone.

"Yeah," she confirmed. "A cop. Which means he's never home. And when he is he doesn't even know I'm there. For the last year, I've been fucking myself almost every day while creepy Internet trolls watch me and tell me to shove who-knows-what into every hole I've got." Maria had moved forward and was straddling Brent's shins. She reached back and unclasped her bra and then tossed it off to the side.

"But, what if he finds out? Cops can do things. Like, arrest people. Or shoot people," Brent tried to reason with her.

"He's not going to find out. Do you know why? Because one, you didn't use your real name," she said as she slid closer towards him. "And two, that's not my car in the parking lot." With that Maria had moved her panties against Brent's crotch.

The head on top of Brent's shoulders was silently screaming, Run, you fool, run. Run before you die. But the head between his legs had decided to veto that action, as it was now standing at full attention. Brent grabbed Maria by the waist and rolled her over onto her back. With a quick, well-practiced motion he had removed her panties and was pressed on top of her, caressing every inch of her body and giving her every inch of himself. Before the night was over he had finished more times than ever before, and Maria claimed she had lost count of her own orgasms. He noticed sunlight had started to appear through the closed and tattered blinds just as he fell into a well-deserved slumber.

Brent awoke a few hours later, reaching over to pull Maria towards him. Instead, he clutched at the air. He looked towards the bathroom but the door was open, and the lights were off. He turned on the lamp that was next to his bedside and quickly noticed that all of Maria's belongings were gone. On the table in the corner, he saw a piece of paper. He stood up, stretched, rubbed his eyes, and then walked a few steps over to investigate. Written in beautiful female cursive was a note on stationary that appeared to come from the front desk.

*Thank you. I feel alive again. I thought I was dying but you saved me. Last night was the best night I've had in a very long time. I wish you the best, George Brenson.*

*xoxo*

*LatinGoddess94*

### **Venality** - *(vee-nal-i-tee)*
Willingness to take bribes or sell one's services for the purpose of advancing a personal agenda

**D.T.:** *Here.*

The gates to Tymborlyn Manor opened, and an unmarked police car pulled onto the property. The Tymborlyn estate sprawled over roughly 60 acres of land near the East Bank District in White River City. A wildlife preserve was abutted to the White River and took up a good portion of the acreage. The northern part of the property consisted of an orchard and a park, both of which were open to the public. Tymborlyn Manor itself was positioned on the south side of the estate. To the east of the property were several smaller houses, though large in comparison to most homes, and a museum that celebrated the history of the Princemoore Family.

The Princemoore clan originally acquired their wealth during the Gold Rush in California. Ezekiel Princemoore initially invested his earnings in real estate, understanding that the prospect of gold would send people streaming into the West. His gamble paid off, and over time he managed to diversify into railroads, coal, and oil as well. His youngest son, Thadeus, was sent to set up operations in the Midwest.

Thadeus ended up choosing White River City for its proximity to several rail lines and canals. Property was also cheap and available, and Thadeus purchased a multi-acre swampland just east of the White River for almost nothing. The draining of the swampland and construction of Tymborlyn Manor was long and arduous, so Thadeus spent a lot of time traveling between White River City and Lake Land Harbor to the north.

## The Virtue of Vices – Jeremy McShurley

After three years the mansion was completed, and over the next decade Thadeus developed the orchard and garden. When large deposits of natural gas were discovered in the 1880s Thadeus summoned his brothers to the area to invest in some factories for the city. But as the gas boom ended, all of the brothers but Thadeus moved onto other ventures. Feeling that he could trust his son Abraham to the family business, Thadeus retired early and spent the rest of his life traveling the world until his death in 1923.

Abraham had three children, Alexander, Morris, and Paulina. When Abraham died suddenly in 1925 at the age of 46, Alexander took over the property while Morris built his own complex in the area that would later become Santa Mesa. Paulina married a German banker named Franz Sauer and moved overseas. She died during the Dresden Bombings of World War II.

The last person to live in Tymborlyn Manor was Talia, Alexander's wife. Alexander died in 1962, and afterward, Talia spent most of her time expanding the family's philanthropic activities. Her daughter, Rebecca, married a man named Carey Porter and showed no interest in the family business. After Talia's only son, Raymond, died unmarried and childless, Princemoore University and the White River Historical Society took over the management of the property. Talia Princemoore passed away peacefully in her sleep in 2002 at the ripe old age of 96.

**D.T.:** *Where are you?*
**PeteP:** *In the garden by the centaur*
**D.T.:** *Be right there.*

Peter turned around at the sound of rustling behind him. The flash of a lighter showed the face of

## The Virtue of Vices – Jeremy McShurley

Detective Terrance Tranche, cigarette held between his lips.

"What'd you do this time, Pete?" asked the detective in his low, raspy voice. He blew a cloud of smoke into the air.

Peter Princemoore was straddling the back of a large centaur statue that stood towards the rear of the Tymborlyn garden. He was leaning forward, hugging the back of the upper, human portion of the mythological beast. "It was an accident," was all Peter answered.

Detective Tranche slowly walked towards Peter, his feet crunching on sticks and the few leaves that had already fallen to the ground this season. "You drunk?" Tranche asked.

Peter didn't respond.

"High?" prodded the detective.

"I didn't mean to," was Peter's response.

Tranche dropped his cigarette into the damp grass and snuffed it out with the heel of his boot. He was still dressed in his work clothes; a black suit with a red tie. He almost always wore a matching fedora, not for fashion, but to hide the growing bald spot on the back of his head. On his belt were his badge and a holster carrying his 9mm pistol. The weather earlier in the day had been unusually warm for the time of year, and a low band of fog had started to form over the ground. He traced his thumb against the bottom of his peppered goatee, then dragged his thumb and index finger up and rubbed them across his mustache.

"What didn't you mean to do, Petey?" Detective Tranche had come to Peter Princemoore's aid more times than he could count. He knew he was enabling Peter's actions, but Tranche didn't really care. The kid was loaded and would pay anything to avoid getting arrested or keeping his name out of the newspaper. Of course, Uncle Sam had no idea about their secret transactions, as Tranche only took cash for his services.

"Oh, Terry," Peter started, referring to the detective by his nickname. What began as a couple of light sniffles quickly escalated into long, deep sobs. If anyone had been nearby, they might have thought a cow was giving birth.

It had been almost twenty years since Detective Tranche had heard Peter wail like that. The last time he could remember was when Peter broke his arm falling out of a tree while playing hide-and-seek. It was during Memorial Day weekend. The entire Princemoore clan had been summoned to Tymborlyn to celebrate the holiday. Even a few distant relatives made the journey that time. Peter came running up to the back porch holding his left forearm. His face was pale and his eyes were glazed over in shock. His mother, Vanessa, asked him to show the wound, thinking it was only a scratch. Instead, Peter revealed a compound fracture. She immediately turned as white as Peter and fainted onto the cobblestone porch. A few of his aunts began screaming, which brought Peter out of shock, letting him feel the pain of his injury.

Tranche, still just an officer then, tore off his shirt and wrapped the wound. He picked up Peter and carried him to his cruiser. Peter's father, Karl, Jr., ran behind, and helped lay Peter down in the back seat, then jumped into the passenger's side. Peter's crying caused Karl, Jr. so must distress that Tranche turned on the sirens just to drown out the young boy's screams of agony. This early Saturday morning, Peter made those noises again.

Detective Tranche gently patted Peter's leg. He then reached up and pulled Peter off the statue and gave him a bear hug. Tranche could feel the snot drip onto his neck, and Peter's sobs began to settle down.

"I fucked up, Terry. I fucked up really bad this time," Peter confessed as he backed away from the embrace and leaned his back against the centaur statue.

Tranche handed him a handkerchief, which Peter used to blow his nose. "Wreck the new car? Get another bitch pregnant? Got in a bar fight? What?" Tranche questioned, each time only receiving a silent headshake.

"She's inside," Peter finally revealed. He led Detective Tranche to the front door and slowly opened it up. He stood there, waiting for Tranche to go in first.

The last time Detective Tranche had set foot in Tymborlyn Manor was in 2000 for Madam Talia's 94th birthday. His friendship with the Princemoores had come by complete accident. The only reason he had been at the Memorial Day gathering was because his partner had eaten some bad oysters the night before and couldn't be there. Tranche went in his stead. The family had been receiving death threats for starting a new subdivision over an Indian burial ground, so they decided to hire an off-duty cop to keep an eye on them until the situation subsided. After rushing young Peter to the hospital, Tranche was adopted into the clan, enjoying all the amenities his new position offered.

The foyer was dark, but Tranche knew his way around, having been in the manor numerous times. He started shining his flashlight around the room, stopping when his light shone on the body. She was lying on her back just a few feet away from the large rug that sported the family crest. Tanche heard the door close behind him as he approached what appeared to be a young woman, her lifeless eyes pointed towards the chandelier above. There was a pool of blood that had gathered beneath her skull and ran into a stream a couple of feet long. Small speckles of red dots were scattered in a circle around her head.

"I didn't mean to," Peter said, standing behind Detective Tranche. He had calmed down considerably since their earlier encounter.

"I know you didn't, Petey. You never mean to," Tranche answered in his gravelly voice. "What happened? I need to know, if we're going to clean this up."

Peter told Tranche what happened. Peter told him how he'd gone to party at Caligula's Parlor. Peter told him how he paid Kameron over one thousand dollars to come back with him for a private show. Peter told him how they went upstairs to the bedroom. Peter told him how he couldn't get it up. Peter told him how he got angry and they struggled. Peter told him how he pushed her; too hard. Peter told him how he tried to grab her. Peter told him how it sounded; like when he was a kid during the Fourth of July, and he would smash watermelons with a baseball bat. Peter told Tranche everything.

Detective Tranche shined the flashlight up towards the second story balcony. He visualized the poor girl falling backward, her pathetic stripper life flashing before her eyes. From her looks, she was probably a college student. He prayed that she wasn't; those were the one's people gave a shit about.

Tranche felt a little sorry for Peter. He wasn't the brightest bulb in the pack, but he could talk his way out of almost anything. As long as Peter followed all of Tranche's instructions, he might not get life in prison. He had watched Peter grow up, since their first encounter when Peter was only ten years old. Tranche knew early on that Peter was going to have issues. His older brother, Scott, was the star in Karl, Jr.'s eye. Peter did his best to garner attention, but the second son plays second fiddle, especially among the affluent. The Princemoores were a different breed. Born into a reality that was so distant from the truth, they wouldn't know how to survive a day without their bank accounts, servants, or country clubs. And Detective Tranche had been playing them all since day one.

Terrance Tranche never had dreams of becoming a cop. He wanted to become President of the United States. While the spitballs and shouts of "faggot" struck him from behind in school, he drew up his plans. He had entered high school at the beginning of the Reagan Revolution. It was at that time when he joined the Young Republicans and ran for student council, winning his junior and senior years. He could have signed up for the Army after graduating, but it was during the Cold War, and the police academy seemed like a better fit. It was the first step in his goal of reaching the highest office in the land.

Tranche knew he would have to work his way up the political ladder. He needed several things to do so; money, contacts, and a reputation. The reputation came from his service on the force. He could have run for local office and perhaps state legislature, but there was always the chance of a political misstep, especially at that young age. Instead, he hustled as a beat cop before attaining the rank of sergeant at the age of 25. He donated to local campaigns and volunteered to handle security for various fundraisers, all the while learning the in's and out's of the political world. After rushing young Peter to the hospital, the Princemoores put in a good word, and he became a detective before he was thirty.

As Peter got older, Tranche watched him fall in with the wrong crowd time and time again. Whenever he got into trouble, Tranche would come to his aid. After Peter turned eighteen and gained access to considerable resources, he began to take payments, passing them off as bribes for his superiors. But in reality, Detective Tranche had kept the money himself. He had gained access to the resources required to fund his future campaigns. Tranche had worked out a formula, figuring he could leave the force and run for Congress in 2020 based on Peter's pattern of destruction. After this most recent faux pas, Tranche planned on retiring early.

"Ok, Petey. I need you to go to the garage, grab all the tarps you can find and wrap up our friend real good, ok?" he commanded.

Peter stood, silently staring at Kameron's cold corpse.

"Come on," Tranche clapped. "Chop, chop."

Peter snapped out it and followed the orders.

Detective Tranche walked upstairs and checked the condition of the banister. It appeared to look undamaged, so he proceeded to the security room. He picked the lock then sat down at the terminal. While not a computer genius, he had plenty of experience with camera systems. He turned the cameras off then deleted the entire day's recordings and replaced the files with the one's from the previous day. He then set the computer to run a maintenance check until the following afternoon. Tranche then walked into the bedroom and gathered all of Peter and Kameron's belongings, placing them in a trash bag.

Peter was just finishing up with wrapping the body when Detective Tranche came down the stairs. "Good work, Peter." He next had Peter help him move the corpse to the trunk of his car and then returned to the foyer.

"Take off your clothes," Tranche told Peter.

"Why?" Peter asked.

"Take them off then put them in here," he again ordered, holding out the trash bag.

Peter reluctantly did as told.

"Now, find some bleach and start scrubbing," the detective ordered, pointing to the blood stained floor. "I'll be back in just a bit."

Detective Tranche drove the short distance to his house where he picked up a pair of sweatpants and a t-shirt. He then drove to an alleyway at the University Mall, where a gunman had recently killed several victims in a coffee shop called the Beanstalk Cafe. When Peter contacted him over an hour ago, Detective Tranche had left, claiming to be following up on a lead. The investigation was still ongoing, and Tranche was able to blend right back in.

The forensic team was currently working the inside of the building. Out front, several officers were still questioning some witnesses. Tranche returned to the alley and opened the trunk of his car. He unrolled the tarps then scanned around to see if anyone was looking. Once he made sure the coast was clear he opened a nearby dumpster and heaved Kameron's corpse inside. Detective Tranche knew that the investigation would keep the area cordoned off for several days. This time of year the body wouldn't start smelling until the next day. Once discovered, he would take charge and ensure that the case never saw the light of day; just another poor stripper who wandered down the wrong street at the wrong time.

## The Virtue of Vices – Jeremy McShurley

    The detective slowly strolled back to the front of the shop where he noticed some news crews. He was tempted to make an appearance but remembered he still had some unfinished business at Tymborlyn. A uniformed officer approached him.

    "What a shame," the young cop noted.

    "A tragedy. Worst shooting in years," Tranche replied, pulling out his cigarettes. He offered one to the officer, who declined. "Yeah, I should probably quit too," but instead he lit up.

    Over the radio came in a report of a potential sighting of the Beanstalk suspect heading south on Highway 17. The officer looked at Detective Tranche, as though awaiting permission.

    "Well, go!" he ordered. The officer sprinted off to his cruiser, waited for his partner to get in, then turned on his lights and sirens and sped away in pursuit.

    Detective Tranche made one last pass through the crime scene. He signed a few reports, and then announced he was headed out for the night. He returned to Tymborlyn to find Peter still cleaning the floor with bleach.

    "That should probably do it, Petey," Tranche informed him. "Here, put all that stuff into the bag," he said, indicating the cleaning supplies. Again, Peter silently complied. Tranche then handed Peter the clothes he had picked up from earlier. "Here, put these on."

    Tranche headed down into the basement. He went into the corner and opened the door of an old wood-burning heater. The detective then placed the trash bag inside and started the fire. Once he was certain everything was burning hot, he closed the door and walked back upstairs. He found Peter sitting on an antique Victorian-era fainting couch that was set back in the corner of the foyer.

"I'm not a bad person. I just do stupid things," he said looking into the darkness of the manor.

"I know, Petey, I know," Tranche gently patted Peter's right cheek. "Now, you said you left the club around 1:30?" he asked.

"I think so. Around there, yeah," Peter agreed.

"And people saw you with Kameron?"

Peter nodded.

"Ok, this is what happened," Tranche began. "You left and went driving around like you said. Then, she got a little weirded out, and she asked you to take her back to the club. While you were driving through campus, she told you to stop, then she jumped out. That's the last you saw of her. You got it?"

Again Peter nodded.

"It's going to be alright, Peter. I've spoken with my friends at the station. But, it's gonna cost you."

"How much?" Peter asked.

"Two million," Tranche responded.

"Two? Million?" Peter's face went ashen.

"I know. I tried to talk them down. But this isn't a speeding ticket. You don't have to pay it all at once. But they need it by the end of the year. Can you handle that?" Detective Tranche asked.

Peter sat and thought for a minute. "Yeah. I can handle it."

"Good boy," said the detective, patting Peter on the shoulder. "Why don't you take yourself a nice vacation? I'm thinking. Vegas!"

The Virtue of Vices – Jeremy McShurley

**Wastefulness** - *(weyst-fuhl-nes)*
Mindless or careless expenditure of one's own time or resources

Laurie was grabbing her leftovers from Pattywack's as she watched her father come out of the apartment building. "That's everything," he stated, having just dropped off several bags of snacks upstairs.

She reached her arms around him and the two hugged. After releasing their embrace she patted him on the stomach a couple of times.

"What was that for?" he asked.

"For luck."

Laurie's dad squinted his eyes in confusion. "Ok, thanks," he said as he got into his car. "Oh, by the way, I left some money on the fridge if you wanna get delivery. You girls have fun tonight. But not too much fun if you know what I'm saying."

"Oh, Dad, gosh," Laurie replied as he drove away. She walked over to the shared mailbox of her dad's apartment complex and opened the box marked 304 with her key. She then grabbed the contents and made her way towards her dad's unit and went inside. As she ascended the stairs to his third-floor apartment, she shuffled through the assortment of deliveries.

"Junk. Junk. Bills. Bills. Oh, whoops." Laurie noticed that one of the pieces of mail belonged to her dad's neighbor. His name escaped her at the moment, but she was almost certain it wasn't Current Resident. That reminded her of a boy she had been talking to who claimed he was going to change his name to Current Resident. He thought that would be a great way to get other people's mail. Laurie had to gingerly explain to him that wasn't exactly how it worked.

After putting the leftovers in the refrigerator and leaving her dad's mail on the kitchen counter, she walked down the hall a couple of doors and knocked at apartment 308. She was just turning to leave when she heard some noise coming from inside and decided to knock one more time. The door slowly opened.

"Yeah," asked an overweight man wearing nothing but boxers and a loosely tied bathrobe. He had thinning red hair and the stubble to match. His nose was large and bulbous, and the lines of wear and tear on his face made him appear older than his actual age. He rubbed his eyes and tried to focus in on whoever was knocking on his door.

"Hi, I'm Paul's daughter from 304. We got some of your mail," she said, presenting him the envelope. Current Resident grabbed it from her hand.

"Oh, pssht," he said, mindlessly tossing onto the floor. He started to close the door, and then opened it back up. "Wait, Paul Kozlowski?" he asked. Laurie turned her head away as the smell of morning breath tinged with booze engulfed her nasal passages.

"Uh huh," she coughed a bit.

Current Resident opened the door all the way. "Come on in. I've got some of your dad's mail."

Laurie accepted the invitation. As she stepped into the apartment's hallway her nose was again invaded by a horrid concoction of unpleasant smells. She tried to place each one, deciding that it was a combination of body odor, rotten food, sulfur, and mold. Laurie pinched her nostrils shut with her thumb and fingers but quickly pretended to be scratching her nose as Current Resident turned around.

"Could you close that behind you?" he asked in reference to the still open door.

Laurie did as asked and slowly walked towards the living room. As she passed the bathroom, she noted a couple of piles of clothes and towels lying on the floor. The sink was covered in grime and whiskers while the toilet itself was caked with something that looked like it had come from a horror movie. The living room was in no better shape and she wondered if Current Resident had ever heard of the concept of a trashcan.

He was in the kitchen going through what appeared to be countless stacks of old mail. Laurie could see a dish filled sink and plates spread about in random piles all over the counter. A large flat screen television sat upon an entertainment center surrounded by numerous beer and soda cans. It appeared to be showing some action movie she guessed was from a time before she was born. Five pizza boxes lay on the coffee table, and Laurie could see that a few of the boxes still contained uneaten slices. In the corner was a recliner covered in newspapers. The only piece of furniture that had any semblance of cleanliness was an old beat up couch with a pillow at one end and a large Afghan wadded up at the other.

Current Resident walked into the living room and over towards the recliner. He picked up the newspapers in one giant stack and tossed them onto the floor next to the chair. Most of the papers looked untouched. She glanced down and noticed that the date on the top paper was from three years ago. She couldn't understand how someone could be so lazy as not to throw away a newspaper from that long ago.

Whoever Current Resident was, it seemed he lived a very sad, unhealthy life.

"Have a seat," he offered.

"Oh, I'm fine thanks. I don't think I'll be here that long," Laurie informed him.

"No, go ahead. I know it's around here somewhere. You want something to drink?" Current Resident grabbed a soda from a box sitting on the ground.

"I'm ok…"

"Think fast," he warned, tossing the can towards Laurie. Surprisingly she managed to catch it right before it smacked her in the face. "Nice catch, you play sports?"

"No, not really." Laurie acquiesced to the fact that she was going to be here for a minute and sat down in the recliner. She was shocked at how comfortable it was and eased herself into the back of the chair as she opened the can. She imagined that if this had been his regular seat, his weight would have mangled the springs long ago. Although the stack of newspapers that had once rested on the chair had put her off, she was glad for its apparent disuse.

"No sports, huh? You more into that nerd stuff then?" asked Current Resident, apparently unaware or uncaring of the insulting tone of his voice.

"I don't know. I'm in honors classes. And I'm on the debate team and treasurer of the Science Club." Laurie laughed at the description of her activities. "So, yeah, nerd stuff."

Current Resident had moved to yet another pile of junk in his attempt to find Paul's mail. Laurie sat in silence as she watched him dig through what was mostly trash. Again her eyes were drawn towards the pizza boxes. She couldn't be for certain, but it looked as though one of the pieces of pizza had a layer of black and white fuzz growing on it. Her gag reflex kicked in so she took a big slurp from her pop and set it on the end table next to her chair.

Laurie noticed a photo of Current Resident in a police uniform standing next to another cop. In her wildest imagination, she would have never assumed that Current Resident was a policeman. Then again, her stereotypes of law officers came from watching television and movies. Every once in awhile one of the local police stations would send cops to her school to give a presentation about staying off drugs, keeping safe at night, or how to deal with an emergency. But no one like Current Resident had ever shown up, and she wondered how he would be able to chase down a suspect if he ever had to.

"Is that your partner?" she asked, pointing to the picture.

Current Resident turned around. "Yeah, that's him. Officer Grant 'Goody Two Shoes'," he snidely replied.

Laurie was a bit taken aback by his candor. "You make that sound like a bad thing."

He chuckled, "Nah, I'm just busting his balls. We've been partners for, what, five years now. Being around someone all the time, it gets a little, I dunno…"

"Blasé," she suggested.

Current Resident nodded. "Yeah, blasé. You are a little smarty-pants, aren't you? You gonna grow up and be a scientist someday, little miss treasurer?"

"I was thinking about botany. Or one of the other earth sciences," she explained.

"Botany. Isn't that plants?" Current Resident had made his way back into the kitchen again as he began to search through the drawers.

"Yes."

He looked up. "How the hell are you gonna make any money working with plants?"

"Science isn't about the money. It's about searching for the truth," Laurie informed him.

"Well, speaking of the truth, I think I just found your dad's mail," Current Resident confidently exclaimed as he pulled a few pieces of mail from out of one of the kitchen cabinets. "It's always the last place you look."

"Even if it's the first place you look it's still the last place," she commented as she stood up and walked towards Current Resident.

He shook his head as he handed her the mail. "You sure don't think like the rest of 'em. I wouldn't mind chatting some more, but I gotta get ready for work."

Laurie quickly glanced at the addresses to make sure everything was in order. "Thank you," she said as she walked to the entryway.

"Tell your dad I said hello," Current Resident requested.

"Sure." Laurie closed the door behind her, relieved to be out of that mess of an apartment. It wasn't the clutter that bothered her. Anyone who had been in her room would know that to be true. It was the filth that had made her feel uncomfortable. Although she had bathed earlier in the morning at her mom's, she felt a desire to shower off whatever mold and bacteria might have been covering the surfaces of Current Resident's home. As she walked back to her father's place, she decided that the next time she found Current Resident's mail she would just slip it under the door.

    Laurie added the new mail to the stack from earlier. As the images of Current Resident's bathroom played over and over in her mind, she shuddered and again decided that a shower was in order. Once cleaned up she started going through the bags of snacks her father had purchased earlier in the day. There was far more than she and her friends could consume in one evening, and she had a feeling she would be snacking on this haul for her next several visits.

    It was still several hours before her friends would be arriving, so she decided to clean up the place a little bit. Her father had already done a decent job, and her efforts were more of a time killing device than a critique of the apartment's cleanliness. First, she finished up what few dishes were left in the sink, and then proceeded to vacuum the living room. After that, she decided to put some time into cleaning the bathroom. While it might have met the typical bachelor's standards, Laurie knew that the six girls she was having over for the evening would probably have a problem with its current state. She considered fixing up her room but instead grabbed a few items and left them in the living room where they would be spending most of the night.

    Laurie sat down on the couch and was just about to grab a book when she noticed a message on her phone.

    **Kyle H.:** *Gimme a call when you get this.*

Having nothing better to do, she decided to oblige the request. The phone rang a couple of times before picking up.

    "Hello?"

"This is Laurie. You said to give you a call?" Laurie felt a little nervous, as she wasn't certain of Kyle's intentions. He was a freshman at Santa Mesa High, and the two had been introduced through a mutual friend over the summer at the bowling alley, Penny Lanes. For a few weeks, they were able to see each other on a regular basis. But once school started it became more difficult to get together. They stayed in contact over the phone or through instant messaging, but she was beginning to worry he was losing interest.

"You at your dad's this weekend?" he asked.

"Yeah, but I'm sort of having a girl's night," she let him know.

"Girl's night. That sounds awesome. Can I come?" he asked as his hormones kicked into second gear.

"Are you a girl?" Laurie kicked her feet up onto the coffee table.

"Uh, no," he responded after a slight pause.

"Then I guess you can't come," she laughed. "But maybe we can do something tomorrow night."

"Sounds awesome. I think *Demon Stalker II* is playing at the MegaPlex," he suggested.

Not being one for horror films, Laurie decided to mention a romantic comedy. "Maybe. I've been wanting to see *When it Rains it Pours*."

"Yeah, yeah," Kyle answered a bit disappointed. "I think I heard of that. Do you just want to meet up there?"

"I'll see if my father can drop me off. Call you tomorrow?"

"Ok. Talk to you then," he agreed.

"Bye," she hung up before dragging the conversation out any further. The fact of the matter was that she wasn't even sure her father would agree to such a date. He didn't have a problem with her going to the movies with a group of kids, but this would be the first time she would be going by herself with a boy. It wasn't that he was overprotective. It was just that she had never been in this situation before and had no idea how he might react to the idea.

It was also very possible that her father would be all for the idea. The weekends were some of his most lucrative days of the week if the Fates happened to be on his side. During lunch, she had caught the beginning of a conversation he was having with his bookie. From the sound of it there seemed to be some sort of a misunderstanding, and he disappeared for almost half an hour to take care of business. From his demeanor upon returning it appeared that everything had been worked out and the two enjoyed the rest of the afternoon together.

Laurie's mom, though, was nothing at all like her father. While he was always looking to make the next big score she worked diligently to provide a stable source of income for the family. And even when he would win big one week it would all be gone by the next. Paul Kozlowski never seemed to fully grasp the concept of money. It was more some sort of intangible and abstract mirage, shimmering in the distance only to end up being nothing more than another pipe dream.

It was her father's frivolous lifestyle that most likely pushed Laurie towards the sciences. Science was concrete and able to be validated. You couldn't just go with your gut or throw darts at a wall to get your results. Science was a process that took dedication to a hypothesis and the belief that methodology trumped ideology.

Laurie suddenly remembered about *The Leon Joneway Show* marathon. She had been listening to it earlier in the day, but her father had changed the station. She opened a bag of chips, turned on the radio, and sat back on the couch, flipping through magazines as it played in the background.

*"...parasites sucking off the government's teat. The American Dream is if you work hard, save your money, and plan for the future that nothing is impossible. But there are too many Americans who want to sit at home and watch TV, taking the hard earned cash out of other's hand."*

*"That's not fair putting everyone who's on government assistance into the same box. Most people want to work. And if given the opportunity they would. We just don't have the jobs available for everyone. There are single mothers and fathers out there who are working two, sometimes three jobs and still need to go on food stamps. For the most powerful and wealthy country in the world, that is unconscionable."*

*"Because the corporate tax rate is too high. If the President would work with Congress to pass tax reform, then there would be more jobs created. Instead of taking taxpayer money to buy drugs and gold chains those people would be adding to the coffers."*

*"I don't really like how you keep referring to people in need as 'those people.' They have names. Like a single mother named Connie I met a couple of weeks ago. She doesn't have a car, so she takes the bus or walks to work. She has two part-time jobs, no insurance, no benefits, and three young children. But she doesn't complain. She doesn't whine. She tries her best to provide for her family. And all she asks*

*for is a little respect and some assistance to buy clothes for her kids and put food in their stomachs."*

*"Then get another job. It's not that hard. Maybe she should try going back to school. Or maybe she should have stopped at child number one."*

*"Well if your party didn't cut funding for free contraception, or spent more resources towards sex education, then maybe Connie and women like her wouldn't be in that situation."*

*"It's not the government's job to tell people how to live their lives. Take responsibility for yourself and quit being a drain on everyone else."*

*"A drain? You keep talking about parasites. How about the billions of dollars that American corporations have locked away in offshore accounts? Shouldn't that be going towards things like job creation instead of executive bonuses? And besides, most of these companies end up paying zero in federal taxes because of a skewed system. We need..."*

Laurie turned the radio off and answered her phone. "Hello? Hi! Yeah, he got, gosh, all kinds of junk for us tonight. I know! Me too. He's going to be gone most of the night. But he left us money for dinner. Pizza? Actually, right now the thought of pizza kind of makes me sick."

**Zealotry** - (*zel-uh-tree)*
Uncompromising devotion to a certain religious, political, or other ideological belief

Justin stared lovingly at the picture of his deceased mother. Memories of her warm, gentle smile and soothing manner formed a layer of shimmering tears across his bright blue eyes. He needed her now more than ever, but her passing seven years ago made that impossible, at least in the flesh. Justin knew she was watching him from Heaven, with Lord Jesus by her side, and he felt the Holy Spirit guiding his hands and giving him the will to carry on. The days he would come home from school, bruised both mentally and physically from the constant taunts and tortures of the bullies and jocks, were far behind him. Yet he could still hear the nurturing and understanding voice of his mother as she reassured him that everything would be alright.

Mrs. Harlowe's last will and testament had left her entire estate to Justin, including the house in which he was currently standing. Justin was an only child, and Mrs. Harlowe had been a single mother since her husband left his family for a man named William Cooper when Justin was only four years old. Over the years father figures came and went, but none of them were able to heal the emotional wounds that had cut Mrs. Harlowe's heart so deeply. Justin never had the opportunity to reconcile with his father. Mr. Harlowe died from AIDS when Justin was still in middle school. And the paternal replacements of his mother's dating life were tainted with such brevity and turmoil that Justin gave up on being someone's son long before he had become a man of his own.

The sounds of the cuckoo clock in the living room brought Justin out of his reverie. He gently set his mother's picture back down on the dresser in his old bedroom and shuffled his way towards the clock's artificial chirps, arriving just as the tiny, carved bird made its twelfth brief appearance, then disappeared back into its home for another hour. Directly underneath the clock was a wooden three-legged table with a white, lace tablecloth and a green, antique lamp set upon it. Justin pulled open a small drawer on the table and removed the clock's crank key. The clock had belonged to his great-grandmother and was by far the oldest item in the house. Everyday at midnight he would crank the weights of the clock back into position, giving life once again to the family heirloom. For generations a member of his mother's family had performed such a simple, yet necessary task. For a moment he wondered if this might be the last time that would happen.

 Justin turned and looked around the dimly lit living room. Since his mother's death he had not changed a single thing, leaving it to serve as a museum to her memory and a reminder of better days. A green, felt love seat sat in front of the large bay windows that opened to the front yard. The curtains had been drawn shut for many years, keeping out both the sunlight and any curious eyes. In the corner sat a wooden rocking chair, a knitted blanket folded and laid over the frame to cover the wear and tear of its woven cane back. An enormous Persian rug covered much of the room's hardwood floor. Its myriad of colors and patterns distinctly matched the motif of the room. Even the bedrooms remained unaltered, as Justin had moved his personal living space into the basement following the funeral.

 A while back he had to replace the refrigerator but otherwise the first floor of the house was in pristine condition, just the way his mother would have wanted it to be. Justin didn't spend a lot of time in this part of the house, and usually, when he did, it was to seek solace. Otherwise, he would cook himself a meal, shower, or use the toilet.

It was downstairs where Justin spent most of the day, reading, praying, or working on his projects. After his mother's death, he had entered a period of dark solitude. The rest of his extended family lived far from White River City, and despite several relatives offering to let him move in, he chose to remain in his childhood home. He had always had trouble making friends, keeping mostly to himself for much of his life. All of that changed when Justin was introduced to Pastor Laura Butler, who then introduced him to Lord Jesus.

Three years ago Mother Laura, as she preferred to be called, had gathered her growing Flock in the center of the West Quad on Princemoore University's main campus. The church was called New Brimstone Ministries, and as the name would suggest, its message was one of fanatical redemption. By sheer chance, Justin had decided to take an alternate route home from his job at the Beanstalk Cafe, located in the University Mall just east of campus. While he hadn't been raised in a strictly religious home, he did go to church with his mother on occasion, especially on Christmas Eve and Easter. After she died he quit going altogether as he slowly slipped into a period of agnosticism and doubt.

Justin was easily drawn towards the crowd of onlookers, many of whom held signs of either protest or proclamation.

"All Fags Will Burn!!!"
"Jesus is Love Not Hate"

## The Virtue of Vices – Jeremy McShurley

"Repent Before the Rapture"
"Forgive the Sinners"
"Go Home Muslims!"
"Love Thy Enemy as Thyself"
As a child, Justin had been a bit of a troublemaker, spending quite a few Saturdays in detention. His teachers and counselors attributed his actions to his family life and they did their best to tame his wild side. As he got older, the fires of mischief became nothing more than the embers of disenchantment, but slowly approaching the growing crowd, he felt the flame of his youthful passions once again ignite.

Despite the occasional retort from disapproving onlookers, Mother Laura's powerful and sturdy voice carried through the air towards the ears and minds of believers and detractors alike.

"None of us, not one single person on God's great Earth, is without sin," she articulated with several finger jabbing motions towards the crowd. "That sin comes from one place, and one place alone, and that is the deep, dark bowels of Hell, whose master is The Father of Lies, The Great Deceiver, the Fallen Angel known as Satan! It was Satan who tempted Eve, who in turn corrupted her husband, Adam, and brought sin into The Garden by their disobedience of God's Law."

"Go fuck yourself, you crazy bitch!" yelled some nameless student from the crowd. After a smattering of laughter, Mother Laura continued.

"This is exactly what I'm talking about. The words of Satan coming out of the mouth of the Children of God." Mother Laura scanned the crowd, looking towards the direction of her heckler. Unable to locate him, she continued.

"The world we live in is one of constant struggle, as we strive against the temptations of the Dark One. But because of His love for us, His most prized creation, God sent his only Son to die for our sins, so that we might live forever with Lord Jesus in Heaven. By accepting Lord Jesus into our hearts, by asking Him to forgive us, and by letting the Holy Spirit guide our actions, we can stave off the evils of Satan."

Justin had been baptized as a child, but he really didn't understand what that meant. His old church had taught the basic teachings of Jesus; to love your neighbor, care for the needy, give to the poor, and follow the Ten Commandments. Yet, all those teachings paled in comparison to the preaching of Mother Laura. She was right. Life was a constant struggle. Life was suffering, and there didn't seem to be a reason for any of it. Perhaps it was Satan. It wasn't God who made his father into a Sodomite; it was Satan. It wasn't God who had taken his mother from him so young, it was Satan. It wasn't God who made the bullies pick on him relentlessly as a child; it was Satan! Satan was the cause for all of Justin's pain, and only Lord Jesus could relieve him from his misery.

"Save me, Lord Jesus! Take away my sin and protect me from Satan," Justin cried out as he stumbled forward, feeling the Holy Spirit pulling him towards Mother Laura.

She opened her arms welcomingly, and Justin easily fell into her loving embrace. "Yes, my Child, yes. Lord Jesus hears you," she assured him as she stroked his hair. She looked back towards the crowd, "Lord Jesus hears all of you. Does anyone else suffer? If so, come forward, and accept Lord Jesus into your heart, mind, and soul."

# The Virtue of Vices – Jeremy McShurley

Surprisingly, a good number of students began to walk towards Mother Laura. The sobs of joy emanating from Justin affected quite a few fence sitters, and by the end of the day, the Flock had grown by twenty-two members. They were all taken back to New Brimstone Ministries where Mother Laura personally baptized each one, gently dipping their bodies into the Pool of Cleansing and washing away the grime that The Father of Lies had smeared them with their entire lives.

Justin quickly became one of Mother Laura's most devoted disciples, moving into her Inner Circle in less than a year. Although Justin was less adept at recruiting new members, he was given more and more responsibility over time. He operated the church's websites, led Bible study classes, and had become quite the carpenter, just like his Savior. Mother Laura's Inner Circle consisted of Justin and eleven other church members, known as the Lion's Pride. They alone were privy to the most secretive of Lord Jesus's message, and Mother Laura would reveal her Visions after the rest of the Flock had left service for the night.

"The time has come. Lord Jesus will soon return. The war between Light and Darkness is upon us. As it is written in Isaiah, 'Look, Damascus will disappear! It will become a heap of ruins. The cities of Aroer will be deserted. Sheep will graze in the streets and lie down unafraid. There will be no one to chase them away. The fortified cities of Israel will also be destroyed, and the power of Damascus will end. The few left in Aram will share the fate of Israel's departed glory, says the Lord Almighty'. The civil war in Syria shows this prophecy has come to be. Though He died as the Lamb, He returns as the

Lion. He will face the Armies of Satan, and we shall be by His side!"

The Lion's Pride cheered at the idea of their Savior's return. Mother Laura continued, "We must now prepare ourselves. We must gather supplies, and seek out the weapons to take on the Armies of Satan. While the heathens battle one another in the Middle East, Satan's most devious worshipers live right here amongst us. They hide behind the flesh, but they shall be recognized by their sins," she finished, becoming more and more inflamed with each sentence.

Again, her Inner Circle cheered, having waited many years for The End Times to finally arrive. Her voice now calmed, Mother Laura completed her sermon, "Each one of you will receive a sign. It will be a sign that will leave no doubt that the time to battle against Satan's minions has begun. And you will know these minions, by the stench of their evil and their disregard for Jesus's love."

Justin unlocked the door to the basement, switched on the light, and walked down the stairs into his sanctuary. He stared down at his hands, now washed free of the blood that had mysteriously appeared only a few short hours ago. The miracle Mother Laura had promised finally materialized in the form of Stigmata. Just as Lord Jesus had bled from the wounds in his hands as he was nailed to the cross, Justin too had bled.

The right side of the room contained several tables with a collection of handcrafted wooden objects. Most of the carvings were of figurines depicting various characters and scenes from both the Old and New Testament. Justin's favorites were the Ark, with its pairs of animals walking up a ramp, and of course, his Nativity Scene. He absentmindedly rearranged them as he walked towards his bed. The bed itself was a pile of straw covered in blankets, as he wanted to sleep the way the Disciples had slept. There he fluffed the straw to make sure no bugs or rodents had burrowed into it.

On the other side of the room was a cabinet full of bottled water and dry rations. Each member of the church had been instructed to keep a six-month supply on hand at all times, as the chaos of Armageddon would make it difficult to find food for quite some time. Next to the supply cabinet was Justin's arsenal. He had collected several useful weapons of which he intended to defend himself and the Flock against Satan's evil minions. Having no existing criminal record, it was easy for Justin to acquire several handguns, a couple of hunting rifles, some shotguns, and plenty of ammunition. He had also purchased a few weapons for those who were unable to acquire some for themselves.

A desk sat against the back wall with Justin's computer setting on top. It was here where he updated the church's website and social media pages and participated in various religious forums. While he wasn't the best at recruiting physical members, he did bring in some donations from the members of different Apocalyptical blogs and news groups. He turned on the radio and sat down to do some work online.

*"...liberal agenda. It is the ineptitude of this administration which has led to the current situation. Just this summer, Assad was re-elected, proving that none of the president's policies have stabilized the situation..."*

*"...no, no. Let's not blame President Obama. If President Bush hadn't invaded Iraq in the*

*first place, and then dismantled the Iraqi Army, which became ISIL, we wouldn't have this…"*

*"… so you're saying Saddam should have…"*

*"…no what I'm saying…"*

*"… you prefer dictators over freedom…"*

*"…let me finish. If not for the illegal invasion of Iraq, and Bush's inability to sign the Status of Forces Agreement…"*

*"…which Obama was unable to renegotiate as well…"*

*"… no, no…"*

*"Ok, ok, gentlemen, we have to take a break. You're listening to the 24-hour Marathon of* The Leon Joneway Show; *this is your host, Leon Joneway. For all of you listeners out there, thank you for your calls. Only six hours left before we leave the airwaves but we are still taking calls. My guests, Greg Philmore of the conservative think tank,* Policy for American Values, *and Henry Glennsworth, author of "How to Right the Wrongs of the Right", will be taking your calls when we get back.*

Justin picked up his phone from off the desk and dialed the number for *The Leon Joneway Show*. He had called earlier in the day during the debate on creationism versus evolution and decided to get involved again. Justin didn't listen to much radio other than Leon's show and Christian stations. Most of the music being played over the airwaves was filled with Satan's vile influences and he did his best to avoid it when possible.

"Hello, this is the Leon Joneway Show. What's your question?" asked the call screener.

"Hi. I have a question about Damascus," Justin replied.

"Your name?"

## The Virtue of Vices – Jeremy McShurley

"Justin."

"And where are you calling from, Justin?"

"White River City." Justin began pacing around the basement, as he tended to do when he was on the phone.

"Ok, we're going to put you on hold until after the commercial. And please turn the volume down on your radio. Thank you." The non-offensive sounds of elevator-style music started playing in Justin's ear. After a few minutes, he was connected to the studio.

*"And welcome back. We have a caller on the line. We're speaking with Justin from White River City. What's your question?"*

*"Hello. This is for both your guests. What is the likelihood of Damascus being destroyed?"*

*"Interesting question. I'll go to you first, Henry."*

*"Thank you, Justin. President Obama has been working with not only our allies in the region but also with the Russians..."*

*"...What about Obama's 'red line in the sand'..."*

*"You'll have your chance, Greg. Go on, Henry."*

*"Thank you, Leon. As I was saying, we have to put diplomacy first and work with everyone involved. The entire situation is extremely dangerous, and the conflict could easily spill over into Turkey and possibly Saudi Arabia. But as for your question, I don't believe Damascus will 'be destroyed.'"*

*"But the Assad regime could be destroyed if liberals weren't so wishy-washy on their foreign policy. President Reagan stood up against the Soviet Union through strength and look at the results. President Obama reversed years of achievements*

*from the Cold War. All it would take is for one nuke to get into the hands of ISIS or the rebels and who knows what might happen to Damascus."*

*"So, gentlemen, it sounds like your answer is possible, but not likely that Damascus will be destroyed. Does that answer your question, Justin? Hello, Justin? I think we lost him."*

Justin hung the phone up. Everything was coming together. Satan had allowed the Antichrist to become President of the United States. Now, the Antichrist was preparing for the destruction of Damascus, just as Isaiah foretold. Justin hadn't failed at bringing the students of Princemoore University in Mother Laura's Flock. They would never join because they were Satan's minions disguised as students. The Stigmata from earlier was the sign he had been waiting for. There had been blood on his hands and there would be more in the future. Justin fell to his knees and prayed. He asked the Holy Spirit to flow into him and lead him to the evil. He asked to be given the vision to see through Satan's illusions and be shown his minion's true forms. And lastly, he prayed that his mother would be proud, and that they would be together again soon.

"It is time."

## The Virtue of Vices – Jeremy McShurley

Jeremy currently resides in Merrillville, located in Northwest Indiana. He shares his life with his fiancée, Danielle, their three cats, Sasha, Tuscany, and Mr. Vanderfloof, a hound named Louise, and all the critters in the Genesis Tank. Jeremy is an ordained minister through the Universal Life Church and he attends the First Unitarian Church of Hobart. His spare time is spent working on various artistic projects, covering a wide-range of genres and disciplines. Jeremy also enjoys hiking, camping, reading, bike riding, learning languages, cooking, and live music events.

For more about the author, visit:

tenchimedia.com/mcshurleyportfolio

*Younker & Wuzzle Publishing* is a
Tenchi Multimedia Project

tenchimedia.com

Made in the USA
Lexington, KY
04 July 2019